The Burden of Rage, Lust, Love

BUCHI RAMARAO VELURY

INDIA • SINGAPORE • MALAYSIA

ISBN 979-8-88869-646-0

To,

My daughter Deepti Velury Bakhshi, an Indian-born British citizen who, at the age of forty, has risen to such a corporate pinnacle in the fiercely competitive world that many of us can only dream of. She is the Indira Nooyi of our extended family.

Contents

Acknowledgements

There are so many people who have motivated, inspired, and shared their knowledge to help me write. This book would not have seen the light of day without their efforts. As a result, recognising any one person would be unjust. I thank them all, as well as Google and its subsidiaries.

I am grateful to the Indian Electrical Engineers for their outstanding efforts in ensuring grid integrity, which has aided the country's progress. I took a few liberties with their workplace culture to fit my fictional story. I apologise and mean no disrespect to their labour.

In addition, I would like to thank the Editorial Team at Notion Press for their diligence in working through my manuscript.

Prologue

Venkatraman climbs the stairs to his daughter's room. As he enters, he glances around. A corridor leads to the room from the stairs, with her slippers chaotically left outside the corner shoe rack. It gave the impression that she had left in a hurry. Venkatraman had not ventured into his daughter's room for almost a decade since she became a teen. Lalitha, his wife, forbade him. She said girls need privacy, so entering an adult female's room is not wise. Occasionally, when she was unwell, Lalitha tended to her. She is a lovely child with a wide-eyed eagerness to learn and trotted along with Venkat as if her life depended on his acceptance of her conduct.

But today is different—a compulsion.

He finds the door ajar, pushes and enters. Looks around thoughtfully. He surveys the room, finds the partly drawn curtains of the French door that separated the room from the balcony. Morning sun sneaks through the recess of the linen curtain, drawing a line of light across the bed set parallel to the balcony. The bed is covered with a light blue satin duvet neatly tucked on all sides. *'Mother's daughter.'*

The door to the bathroom stands open. Venkat peeps in to find a saree, a blouse, and a petticoat chaotically hung on a cloth hanger rod.

He recognises them. They are the clothes Kaveri wore when his cousin and wife from New Delhi came to meet them on their way to a wedding reception in Bengaluru. She was about to go out when he stopped her from leaving the house as his cousin was coming to visit them. They had not seen her since she was in her teens. She said she had an important engagement with a friend and requested Venkat to excuse her. But Venkat did not relent. He asked her to stay for at least half an hour as they were expected anytime. Lalitha also convinced her to stay put and asked her to change from her jeans to more appropriate attire. Finally, she agreed, 'for only half an hour, appa.' But Venkat managed to keep her longer by drawing her into conversations with the visiting couple about her younger days with her cousins in Chennai and New Delhi.

At the opposite end of the balcony is a writing table with a laptop on one side, and the rest has well-arranged writing instruments. Venkat sees the flickering of the Wi-Fi-router next to the table on a stool. A chair with arms smugly tucked under the table.

Closets all around the room are shut except for one. Venkat notices that it is filled with jeans and tops of various colours. He opens a drawer, and it is full of ice-popsicle sticks painted neatly with flags of different countries and some in random but pleasant shades. She had the habit of collecting ice cream sticks from a very young age. He walks into the balcony drawing the curtains.

He imagines her waving him off from the balcony whenever she hears his car move out of the garage. It was her routine from a very young age. On the days she was sick and could not come to the balcony, she insisted her mother escort her to the balcony to wave her appa off wherever he was going. His eyes moisten, reliving the routine.

He doesn't want to peep further into the room and climbs down the stairs to the main hall, where Lalitha is hurriedly moving around hither and thither.

'I am leaving with Subbaih to the hospital and will send him back to pick you up. Please have your breakfast, and after the maid has left, you need to lock the door and come over. The duty doctor and the neurologist are expected to visit the ICU at around eleven a.m.,' says Lalitha and leaves the house, closing the door behind her.

Venkatraman is surprised to note the calmness in her despite the gloom. In contrast, his mind refuses to function. He sighs. He isn't sure how their life will evolve with this unexpected event that has disturbed their peace. Everything appears depressed and confusing. Some restless spirit has disturbed their lives.

He instructs the maid to hurry with her job and has toast and jam, pours coffee from the flask and gulps it as though it is cough syrup. He lungs himself on the sofa to wait for his driver.

He contemplates the events that have transformed the tranquillity of their house.

But for a fastidious cop's search, Venkatraman would not have known that his daughter lay on a hospital bed, not responding to any stimulus by the doctors. They said there was no external injury. Her head must have hit the pavement edge and made her unconscious. They said she was pillion on a motorcycle driven by a young man in his late twenties when the vehicle would have slipped and swirled and hit the car coming in from an adjacent lane. Heavy rain added to the poor visibility, which could be the reason for the accident, the police reported. Later, Venkat learnt that the rider was declared dead upon arrival at the hospital. The cops were trying to find his wallet to inform his kith and kin. The wallet and his mobile were missing in the melee of the accident. They were probably stolen.

Luckily, none noticed his daughter's sling bag flung far away from the road into a drain. The heavy rainwater did not wash away her sling bag, containing her clutch and mobile, and helped the diligent cop notify Venkatraman within two hours of the incident.

Venkatraman rushed immediately to the hospital. He found Kaveri on the bed, immobile. The emergency staff were evasive about the condition of the patient.

We have the routine – standard operating procedure. Medicate the patient. Clean her. Exercise her limbs. Try talking loudly to her so that she may respond. Give shock. Send for diagnostic tests. The whole rigmarole. Beyond that, we must wait for the neurosurgeon to arrive.

Venkatraman noticed a ventilator with a trach tube, vital signs monitor, feeding tube, emergency Oxygen cylinder, and IV med dispenser. He hoped his daughter was in good hands.

He informed his wife, who was distraught on hearing the news and insisted that she visit the hospital. They finally found a responsive white coat, which gave them the medical status of the patient under their care. They were relieved that the accident did not damage her skull or spine and that there could be no permanent damage to her brain.

It has been almost a week; waiting at the hospital lounge has become a routine for the middle-aged couple.

Venkatraman waits for his driver's return to take him to the hospital.

If providence did not kill him, I could have strangled him with my bare hands, being responsible for my Ponni's situation.

PART 1

Chapter 1

My parents were well-to-do. My dad, a lawyer, worked long hours – partly at home and mainly at the High Court. My mom inherited huge acreage in Tumkuru, which my dad sold off, some by force and many by stealth. My parents regularly fought on the property matter. But always, dad prevailed by giving some unintelligible stories of the government takeover of excess land because of land reforms. He cleverly invested the receipts of the clandestine sale in a few shopping complexes around the city, which he had given on rent and that ensured monthly income. Being a lawyer enabled him to take care of a few recalcitrant tenants. He might also have other revenues, which I was not privy to. But he bought expensive clothes and sports shoes for me and never refused my indulgences. My parents lived like parents – not as a married couple. We never went on vacation except for one because of the necessity of attending the wedding of a Judge's daughter in Delhi.

I never had any interest in my studies. I was the school captain of the football, which allowed me to bunk many classes without the need for mandatory attendance for appearing for examinations – internal and external. With athletes, you can see your alternate life a little more clearly. You have the ability to kick the ball just a little faster than the next guy; you end up a GOD of sorts. You get the girls, the fame, and the like. People want to be near you, hear you speak and touch the hem of your sleeve. Academics can take a back seat. I found my passion in the game and soon became popular with boys and girls as I partied with friends – alcohol and other under-the-counter stuff.

One day I passed out drunk, and my friend had to carry me home at 2 am. My mom cleverly sneaked me from the back gate, and I slept until noon, the next day. But the police caught up with us. Somebody talked. That was when dad had to come into the picture. That day the home was like a war zone. He threw every conceivable item on hand – mantel pieces, steel containers, cutlery, you name it – at me. When I ducked, some of them hit mom. He narrated many other incidents that he had to wriggle me out of to justify his anger, like the girl, Anita, whom I tried to kiss on the school lawn to win a bet. Her entire family had come home to confront dad and me. I didn't know what dad had told them, but they quietly walked out. Later I learned Anita got a transfer from our school.

From then on, my dad became different and closely monitored me.

* * *

It was our last semester—no more football matches. Attendance had become compulsory. That was when I noticed Lalitha. 'Pretty' was a small word for her. She wore some exotically coloured dresses, which made her stand out. She was tall by Indian standards, with two plaits, one back and another in the front. I noticed that her dad dropped her to school often. Sometimes she did come by bus. Not knowing her itinerary, I could not watch her movements to befriend her. I learnt that she had only one girlfriend – Tanmai. Her cousin also studied in the same class as ours. I took his help to get introduced to Tanmai with the hope of knowing the schedule of Lalitha. But no luck. My craving for her friendship had no bounds. I was truly besotted with Lalitha. I did say hello to her once in the library when I saw her on the pretext of meeting Tanmai. That was when Tanmai spoke highly of my football skills and how I helped the school ace the championship that year after a gap of over ten years. Meanwhile, the Board exams came in the way of the progress of our friendship, and the school closed immediately after.

I joined a PU college and, having had no interest in academics, was detained in the first year. The college had a reputation for hundred per cent results in the final PU course – Football or no Football. So, they wanted to keep the record intact. 'Dad was upset' is the most understatement of the year. He wanted me to be an heir to his legal profession.

But I wanted time out. I wanted to get drunk, take drugs, and go clubbing. I wanted to do everything my mates would spend the next two years doing. While my mother was feeding me with more rice and dal, I convinced her that the atmosphere there in my college was prejudicial to my growth. All the teachers and the principal had an image of me, and whatever I did would be seen with jaundiced eyes. I needed a sabbatical.

* * *

But my dad had other ideas. He decided to move me to England to pursue a BA (Hons) with Foundation in Law. After the Foundation of one year, I was to enrol on a three-year program graduating in Law. I was not keen on Law or, for that matter, any academic pursuits, as my interests were in football, but I had no alternative. My Chikkappa, an Estate Agent, has convinced me to grab the opportunity as it gives me exposure - "Karthik Maga, it doesn't matter what you like. Take this opportunity and explore the world." Also, I knew that England was a football-crazy country, and I could hone my football skills on the pretext of academic pursuits. It was motivating enough for me to accept the offer of dad. But dad had played a trick on me. The course was in

Scotland, not England, because it was cheaper there. I reluctantly succumbed and moved to Aberdeen in Scotland.

Not having been to a UNIV campus, I was genuinely astonished by the size of the estate the UNIV had. Sprawling campus. Some buildings looked like forts. It gave a heritage feel. But my course was in the modern complex – New King's Tower. The whole university was constructed with the Andrew Carnegie Trust. The budget did not appear to be a problem, as evidenced by the buildings' architectural innovations and visual beauty. I have never seen a sports centre as big. I thanked my uncle for having convinced me to come to this place. The whole of the UK, including Scotland, is football crazy. I thought I would find my calling by joining a football club. But racism came in the way. I wish I had the courage and wherewithal to expose the institutional racism in the clubs – it was not limited to soccer, but in cricket, hockey, you name any team game, racism was prevalent.

I was not allowed to be near any reputed club – even in their B or C teams. I could play a few exhibition matches between our internal student groups in the college. Once, I accidentally went into a private soccer club's dressing room, only to get a dressing down. 'Hey, you GET OUT, GET OUT of here! I told you not to come here – it is an exclusive club of whites only,' that was my college mate! It shocked me. I had to give up my passion and find solace in the other rudimentary pleasures of life. There were so many traps for a pleasure-seeking student in the UK. During recess, I hit the gym and pumped iron.

For a change, I concentrated on my studies too, even though a football match here or a cricket match always lured me. At the end of the year, I got a D amongst many Cs.

* * *

It is a qualifying match for the European Championship between Netherlands and England, shown live in a pub. My friend Zulfi and I went to a pub to watch the game. Scottish football fans are bitter rivals of England, as they lost 2-nil in their previous encounter. But this time, the Scots are rooting for England, along with the English fans, to win so that Scotland could go through on goal aggregate. England was leading 4 – nil and the decibel levels in the pub were at a high pitch. Scots and English are on the same side for the first time, and the number of empty beer bottles in the bins is a testimony. But the last-minute late goal by the Dutch team makes the score line read as 4-1. This score deprives Scotland of a place in the quarter-final. All hell broke loose in the pub. Scots accuse the English of letting the Dutch score a late goal to deprive them of their place in the quarter-finals.

Fist fights ensue. Broken jaws and noses on both sides. I and some of my Asian classmates try to broker peace. Suddenly the mood changes. Scots and the Englishmen start abusing us – the brownies with vile language. One Philippine boy brushes a Scot away as he is being pushed around. Someone called the Police as a siren screeched in front of the door. I, too, got caught in the melee and ended up with a minor cut on the hand – probably by a beer glass piece hurled around. I quietly walk out of the room from the back door.

I notice this girl in nickers and a transparent lace top. She was not part of the group inside the pub. But she appears drunk and visibly lost. Her slippers give away, and she is trying to slip them back. I approach her to help, but she falls on my body, reeking of alcohol. She introduces herself as Claire, says she is lonely and requests me to take her home as she has no money. I try to make her stand erect, and as she leans over my shoulder, I can feel her voluptuous breasts. Suddenly, she hugs me and plants a long and hard kiss. I respond. With a hard-on, I could hardly hold my senses. I try to push my hand through her blouse. She pulls my hand away but continues to kiss me and doesn't try to move out.

'How dare you mess with my girl?' A voice from behind.

Before I could turn around to see who it was, a man put his heavy hand around my neck and twirled me to face him. He is bulky with a vicious look. I try to wriggle out, but he is way too strong. Before I could recover, he delivered a solid punch to my stomach. I collapse. He lifts me, pins me to the wall, and punches me squarely. Blood is oozing around my mouth. I slump to my knees and cover my face to avoid further attacks. All the time, I see Claire giggling. Finally, I hear Claire say, 'Enough,' and she pulls him away from me and walks away with him – still sniggering.

I grimace. I soon realised she used me to take on her boyfriend!

From then on, I never dared to lay my eyes on any invitingly looking girl as long as I was in Scotland. I was allowed to continue attending the main graduation course, provided I cleared the "D" subject within the first year. The authorities appeared simply interested in running education as a business. Whether you are up to it or not. They will not detain you but let you pursue the course with the pending subjects. In India, we call it ATKT However, I was beginning to like the Univ atmosphere. It was so laid back. My dad was happy when I told him about pursuing further studies. He sent the required fee directly to the authorities. He never trusted me with cash. I had to depend on his monthly allowance of fifty pounds. Even hostel fees were also paid directly by him. At home, I had the advantage of my mom topping up my wallet regularly. But she has no access to banks or foreign exchange to help me in this foreign country.

* * *

Some of my friends had decided to spend the weekend in Edinburgh. It was my first visit to the town, though I used its airport to land in Scotland. With a bunch of mates, we watched an India-Pakistan cricket match in a pub. The place was bustling with Indian and Pakistani fans. The game was telecast live from Sharjah on a Friday. By the time the crowd gathered, Pakistan had already scored 266/9. The audience was mostly college students from nearby Dundee, Inverness, apart from Edinburgh. Betting was huge. My Pakistani friend, Zulfi and I started betting. I was betting on Tendulkar, and he was on the match result. Sachin got out for 4.

I lost my first bet. It was then I was introduced to Betwin, a gambling company. Zulfi gave me a complete account of how this company works and how one could make money. My monthly allowance had yet to come. The last few pounds I lost on my first bet. I heard of beginners' luck, but in my case, it didn't prove to be true. Then Zulfi introduced me to Phillip, sitting at the far corner of the pub, nursing a beer. I learnt that he lends money for bets. Zulfi pushed me to borrow and bet. I was initially reluctant, but I was confident of India's win. One cannot go wrong with Tendulkar, Azhar, Kambli, and Sidhu. But India lost. I lost all my savings and the borrowed money too.

Phillip came and consoled me. He said there were many ways to make up. Betwin's site had many opportunities in various sports and gave examples of successes. He did not press for the money he loaned. Instead, he asked me to contact him whenever I wanted to bet. I borrowed and bet. Got addicted. A tenner on a goalie and a twenty on a horse. I won some. But lost much more. My loan amount shot up to 500 pounds. That was much more than the yearly funds that my dad sent me. Phillip's attitude towards me started changing. He wanted the old account to be settled first so I could borrow more and "win".

On a Sunday, I overslept because of heavy drinking at the previous night's party. There was a massive banging on the door. I woke up to open the door. At the entrance were two huge males, six-foot-five and over, with huge biceps. They charged inside my room and pushed me onto the bed. *How did they enter the hostel gates without a proper id?* Before I could react, they started beating me with blows all over my body. My ribs hurt. I thought my kidneys would burst. They finally stopped and said, 'Boss wants you at Clarks at 6 p.m. today.'

My head was spinning. I had to get out of this mess. I must pay the loan shark and quit gambling. But how? There was only one way. Get out of the country. I returned to the Institute and informed the authorities of the breach of security in my hostel without referring to the loan matter. They said sorry and tightened the security. Thus, I could find some respite to think and plan. I did not stir out of the college campus for almost a month – not even for a beer.

Having no other option, I started attending classes regularly. That was when I met Suzanne. There were six of us in what the school called the less-talented group: four boys and two girls. I had nothing in common with Suzanne. She preferred spending lunchtime in the library while I wanted to fag around.

She was different from the other girls. She was shy and always wore various printed knee-length frocks. A couple of times, she sat next to me in the class. After the experience with Claire, I feared girls who volunteered to be near me. But she helped me by prompting answers to the lecturer's queries about the last class. It soon dawned on me why I liked Suzanne. She reminded me of Lalitha. Same two plaits. Same effortless and dainty walk. Suzanne started conversing with me. I opened up to her.

When you are true friends, you talk about everything – the minuses and pluses of your life. She was the only child of wealthy parents in England. They own an estate in Wales and breed livestock – pigs, lambs, and all. In a candid moment, I informed her of my gambling mess and the money I owed to the loan shark. The next day she gave me one hundred pounds and asked me to settle the first instalment. I was not used to this kind of compassion. I hugged her – asexually and thanked her profusely. She smiled and said, 'any time.'

Our hostel compound had a separate entrance from the main road. You could enter and exit the hostel without using the Univ main gate. Most students use this gate for a quick outing. A wicket gate built into a wall that doubles as a border between the Univ and the hostel helped the students move to the Univ main building. University had a separate entrance both for pedestrians and vehicles. I walked past the hostel exit for the first time in a fortnight since the burly gorillas had barged into my room and bashed me up. As soon as I crossed about 200 yards, the same crooks in dark suits started following me. I was going in the same direction they wanted me to, so they had kept their distance. But this image disturbed me. *It is simply difficult to dodge these loan sharks.*

I found Phillip at the usual place in the pub. As soon as he saw me, he smiled and waved to wait at the following table. A lean and petite young man of Asian descent was standing in front of Phillip with a pensive look. From the man's gestures and body language, I noticed Phillip was not inviting the man for an evening drink bash. The man demurely walked away. I approached Phillip and shoved the hundred-pound note into his palm. He was courtesy personified. He did not refer to the visitation of his goons. Instead, he gave me some betting tips and promised me more loans. I refused and assured him that the balance money would be returned soon. But I needed to figure out how to do it. I realised that the Clarks Pub, Phillip and Betwin, were somehow connected to lure students into gambling and get them hooked.

The semester was coming to an end. I had many pending subjects to clear. But the liability of Phillip and his ways of collecting the debt troubled me. Also, I was not sure I would be able to pay back the pending course subjects, even if I spent another four years at the Univ. My bluff would be out in the open after the last semester when the authorities would refuse to give me the required degree certificate unless I completed all the pending subjects.

So, I faked sickness and emotionally blackmailed my mom into calling me back to Bengaluru. Dad had sent the ticket. He believed my visit would be only for a week, and I shall return to complete the course. But getting out of the Hostel without Phillip's thugs cornering me was an obstacle I did not know how to circumvent. That was when Suzanne helped me again. She hired a car, let me lie low in the back seat, and drove me to the airport. You rarely get friends like Suzanne. It was the last time I laid eyes on Suzanne. I was not coming back to the UNIV anyway. I never met her afterwards. After returning to India, I wrote a thank you letter, which was left unanswered.

Chapter 2

'Now for the final award of the year. The outstanding student of the year award ... goes to....'

A portion of the crowd erupts. 'Lalitha Soundar Rajan.'

It had been the tradition of the Seshadripuram Women's College to combine the fresher's day and the valedictory function for the outgoing graduate students of last year. It was held on the first Monday of July every year.

The MC acknowledged the shrieks with a wave of her hand and continued, 'I request Lalitha Soundar Rajan to come to the stage and accept the award.'

The entire audience stood up to cheer, clap and scream as Lalitha walked to climb the podium.

'How many awards have you got?' inquired Sounder Rajan, 'we had come late, and we missed the earlier part of the function.'

Sounder Rajan was driving the car back home after the function with his wife at the back and Lalitha in the front seat.

'Two more – one for cent per cent in Physics, which no one ever got in the history of Bengaluru University, and second was for the best all-rounder student of the college.'

'And you are a dancer of Kuchipudi and Bharatanatyam,' added her mother.

'Amma! They don't acknowledge such skills in our college.'

Lalitha had already enrolled in a PG course and was determined to pursue her passion for academic research in pure sciences. She had to take leave from her professor to attend this function. She was already late for the lab, which was scheduled for the afternoon. She appeared restless.

'Why don't you come home and have some light lunch, and then appa will drop you at the Univ,' said Pavitra.

'No, amma. I am already late. I will eat something at the canteen. Appa, drop me at a point where I can get an auto. You need not drive in this heavy traffic.'

You can't argue with Lalitha.

'What decision have you taken on the alliance proposals for Lalitha?' asked Pavitra, addressing her husband, which made Lalitha look askance at her, turning her head around.

'I already enrolled at the University to pursue my post-graduation in Solid State Physics. Just for your information,' she announced sarcastically.

They spent the rest of the journey in silence. Sounder Rajan was not keen to indulge in any potentially rough dialogue. He wanted his daughter to enjoy the glory of her achievements.

* * *

Lalitha heard a male voice calling her name, and she turned to notice a youth staring at her.

'Hello, Lalitha.'

'Hello.'

'Don't remember me? Karthik, your schoolmate.'

'Yes, how are you?' A polite inquiry.

They exchanged their academic status and parted company that day.

She had been smiling, hadn't she?

Karthik planted himself daily on the street corner to say hello to Lalitha, hoping she would respond. After all, he was from a well-to-do family and had also been to England to pursue higher studies. What more would a girl want?

Lalitha devoutly hoped he wouldn't embarrass her by manifesting himself at the street corner when she would be with her parents. As she descended the bus, she saw him get off at the stop. A less sensitive woman than Lalitha might have assumed that he, too, had come on the bus and alighted at the same bus stop, but she knew better. Lalitha decided that the only wise course was to ignore him. She set off briskly along the colony footpath. Outside the grocery store, she looked around and saw him following. There was nothing to be done about it; she could only hope he wouldn't attach himself to her every time she walked from the bus stop to her home. She was wrong.

The pursuit happened a few more times.

On a Sunday, when Lalitha disembarked from an auto at the front of her home, he rushed towards her and said, 'Lalitha, let us take a walk, for old times' sake.'

'No, I am busy and not interested in boys.'

She walked briskly from the auto without collecting the change.

Karthik would watch her going out of her house and coming in. The more he saw her, the more he was determined to start a conversation. But he could not succeed.

On another day, when Lalitha was walking back from her bus stop to her home, a distance away, Karthik stopped and pulled her towards him. She resisted, but he was strong; he held her hand firmly and dragged her. In the commotion, her bag fell.

'Sorry, Lalitha.'

'Please don't trouble me anymore. I am not interested in you. If I see you near me next time, I have to inform our elders.'

Karthik drew her by her long hair towards him and planted a kiss on her cheek. This infuriated Lalitha. She slapped him hard and hit him with her bag. A fruit cart vendor noticed the disturbance and rushed to save her, and he landed a few blows on Karthik. He saw that some more people were about to join in bashing him up and ran away from the scene.

Would he come after me again? Part of me wished he would, so I could go to the authorities. Better to get it over with than spend God knows how long looking over my shoulder, afraid to walk freely. The day had come sooner than she thought.

* * *

Karthik was wearing sweatpants and a T-shirt, casually tucked. He was waiting at the bus stop and followed Lalitha quietly behind. The evening sun dipped into the sky, and there was a haze in the atmosphere, suggesting the possibility of rain. The road was almost empty except for one or two cyclists riding briskly to their destinations before the rain hit them.

Karthik caught up with her, moved in front of her, stopped her in her tracks, and said, 'You, bitch, you have insulted me in front of every one of my colony. I will not take it lying down. Watch out. I will accost you till you agree to marry me,' he said and did not let her move. She was determined this time to teach him a lesson. She took her bag and took a swing. It missed him.

On the bounce, she lost balance and fell flat on her back. She rose again, took a nearby loose pavement block, and hurled at him. It missed him. He moved towards her to grab her. She moved away and tripped again because her slippers gave out and fell on the uneven footpath.

Blood dripped from her elbow scratch wound. So much so that the trickle might leave a trail when she walked. She stood up to shout at him angrily, covering the wound with her pallu .

He stood there calmly without bothering to help her up.

'I won't let you live in peace. You have to marry me,' he shouted and sprinted off. She stood up with the help of a passer-by, who she recognised as her neighbour, and walked back slowly towards her home with pain in her calves, ache in her chest and fog inside her head.

She was worried about how to explain her wound to her parents. So far, she never shared with her parents these debilitating experiences she was having with this scoundrel. She imagined telling her parents what happened graphically, describing all her encounters with them. This guy came close to molesting her today. Whatever the consequences, she was determined to discuss with her appa all that had happened for the past few weeks. *That would teach him a lesson, wouldn't it, not to force his unwanted attention on her?* She was surprised she still needed to look out for predators in such a homely locality as Malleshwaram, where everyone knew each other.

When Lalitha got home, she quietly went to her room, ducking her paati, who was busy reading the scriptures. She washed and looked in the mirror to see whether any other bruise was visible. None. She changed into a long-sleeved kurta and a Punjabi salwar. And she was waiting for her appa to come from the office.

Paati, realising something was amiss, went up to her room and found her in pain and applying some cream on the wound. When asked what went wrong, Lalitha said she fell while briskly walking because of imminent rain.

Paati took Lalitha to a private clinic. The doctor put a bandage on the bruised hand and said, 'She appears strong enough to me,' he smiled and looked at her reassuringly. The doc took paati to the side and said, 'She does not want to relive the unfortunate experience; please don't press her to give more details that she has already given voluntarily. After a couple of days, when the pain subsides, you ask her to explain the incident further.' Lalitha's mother confronted her, but she was evasive.

After a couple of days, her mother went into Lalitha's room and sorted out her story. She called her appa to be present. She explained briefly about the encounters she had with Karthik.

'You know this guy?'

'Yes, he was my classmate in school.'

'Why did he push you?'

'I slapped him in an earlier encounter wherein he tried to molest me in public.'

'What?'

'He has been troubling me for the past two months; he always finds where I am going, lays siege to my way, and asks me to marry him.'

'Two days ago, he came suddenly in front of me, blocked my way, and tried to kiss me by pulling me towards him. I had to slap him.'

'Why did you not tell us this earlier?' asked Pavitra.

'Every girl has this experience during her time. Nothing new. We have to learn to manage our lives.'

Sounder Rajan was furious.

'Did anyone known to us a witness to all these happenings?'

'Our neighbour Trivedi saw me slapping him and tried to beat the boy. But he ran away.'

Sounder Rajan's neighbour, Angad Trivedi, had taken note of the boy when he first tried to molest her when he came out of his house to see the commotion in the street. Being new to the colony, Trivedi kept the matter to himself until he found Lalitha on the road writhing in pain. And he tried to lift her. He could recognise the boy as the son of Sheshadri, whose bungalow was a few hundred yards away from Sounder Rajan's house.

Sounder Rajan called on Angad and got confirmation of the full particulars of the incident, as witnessed by him. He immediately rushed to the police station and insisted on registering an FIR.

The duty officer of Malleshwaram PS had taken note of the alleged offence and made an entry in the Daily Diary. He wrote down the complaint and asked Sounder Rajan to sign in. The Inspector insisted that as the victim is an adult, she also would have to sign the complaint. Also, they requested that Sounder Rajan prevails upon his neighbour to corroborate the statements made by the father and daughter. Sounder Rajan had to return home to fetch his daughter to take her to Police Station. He also talked with Trivedi, who agreed instantly to help if the Police came to record his statement. 'He moves around the streets like a vagabond. Drives his car with such screeching speed that I was almost thrown onto the pavement a couple of times,' said Angad Trivedi, while recounting the Lalitha's slap incident to the Police.

Pavitra objected to sending her daughter to Police Station.

'Let us bury this incident. Don't make a spectacle of this. Our daughter is unmarried, and I don't want any smear on her character.'

The couple argued on the matter, and finally, Sounder Rajan prevailed. Paati was a silent witness to the angry debate between the couple but did not side with anyone.

The SHO at the Police Station agreed to investigate the matter as soon as possible, and he immediately called his sub-inspector to fetch Karthik, named as the molester in the complaint.

A week after the incident, Sounder Rajan received a message in the form of a letter in his letterbox, unsigned, but on the letterhead of a High Court Advocate, Enniguntla Sheshadri.

'You could have come to me first before going to the Police. I could have reprimanded my son right in your presence. Now you have made serious and false allegations about my son and my family, which are in the public domain. Any legal action by the Police subsequent to your complaint by you would be inappropriate and unreasonable. I would have to seriously consider filing a suit under Sections 499 and 500 of the Indian Penal Code related to defamation. You must withdraw the FIR and apologise to me in my court chambers in front of all my colleagues.'

Enniguntla Sheshadri is a lawyer who practised at Karnataka High Court. He handled everything from family court matters to hard-core criminal cases and earned a reputation for getting things done. A rumour has it that he knew no law or rule – can't differentiate between CrPC and IPC sections. But he is incredibly gifted to manoeuvre a postponement out of the toughest of judges at a crucial point with the idea of starting it once again before a new judge. Sheshadri can manage the bailiff to delay the warrant. Public Prosecutors are often manipulated to either be absent during a vital hearing or make some irrelevant observations. Police Inspectors conveniently miss out on collecting incriminating evidence against his clients.

He had built a palatial bungalow just four blocks away from the house of Sounder Rajan. His son, Karthik, was a schoolmate of Lalitha, the daughter of Sounder Rajan. Karthik acquired all the traits of his father and a little more. He was beaten in school by a girl's brother when she complained that he publicly humiliated her by kissing her on the lawns of their school as a part of a bet.

As per neighbours' gossip, his father, exasperated with his son's antics, had sent him to England for 'further studies.' After four years, he had just returned from wherever he went.

There it was, in black and white. Sounder Rajan was rattled by the letter. He underestimated the fact that he was dealing with an unscrupulous lawyer. Hands trembling, Sounder Rajan kept the letter in his draw and did not find it necessary to share it with Pavitra. His mother has been pushing Sounder Rajan to find an alliance for Lalitha and marry her off quickly. This episode will surely encourage her to drive her agenda.

Chapter 3

My study room suddenly swung open. A tall, pretty girl in her early twenties barged into my room. I had completed checking the SLD, which the substation contractor had sent for approval. I marked a few clouds, wrote the concluding remarks on a sheet, pinned it to the drawing, and got up to close the file inside my briefcase for the next meeting. This girl, whom I knew as Lalitha, thanks to attaih, was standing in front of me.

Lalitha was a lovely-looking woman. I often saw her on the terrace opposite my home, either hanging clothes for drying or removing them after they were dehydrated or reading a book while walking around the periphery of their large deck. Mostly the latter. Studious type. I saw her so close for the first time. I was taken aback by her prettiness. She barely groomed herself. Yet, she looked lovelier than many girls her age I encountered in college and elsewhere. I saw her mostly in Salwar Kameez, with long hair falling until her slightly curved buttocks. She tucks a strand behind her ear ever so often. Beyond that, I had not shown much interest – least of all in marrying her.

Here she was in flesh and blood, charging into my room. She picked the same chair I had vacated to see who had entered my room. There was no other chair except an old sofa with broken springs and a stool that I used to pick up a reference book from my top shelf.

After a few seconds, she gathered her breath and said, 'You know they want us to get married?'

Lalitha thought of the first time she saw Venkatraman. Though he was living in the opposite house, she had not paid attention to the goings-on in the neighbourhood, busy as she was with her academics and dance classes. He was trying to pull out a heavy motorbike across the steep slope of their gate, and the machine slid a couple of times back. He lost balance and tripped. She almost laughed out loud. He did not notice her. That was the only instance she had laid her eyes on his physique. Quite a handsome man. And then she forgot all about him. But now this ridiculous untimely proposal!

'To each other?' I was trying to soften her.

'Don't joke. I am serious.'

'Who are they?'

'Your paati and ...'

'She is not my paati, my attaih,' I corrected.

Attaih is the child-widowed eldest sister of Venkat's father. She looked after the family as a patriarch after the unfortunate demise of Venkat's parents when he was still in his teens. Even though her name was Mangai Ammal, for everyone, including the maids, vendors and neighbours, she was always Attaih.

'Whatever. You better refuse the alliance.'

Then I remembered. Attaih did hint to me about her idea for this proposal. I wondered whether Attaih had a hand in putting the alliance seed in Lalitha's family's mind, as she had been hinting to me about the virtues of Sounder Rajan's family living opposite our home. Lalitha's paati and my attaih were two-body-one-soul buddies.

'I am not aware of what you are saying. Do you mean you want to remain a spinster your entire life? Or are you in love with someone else? Or you don't see me as an eligible husband.'

'No, no, nothing of that sort. It is not our marriage as such, but marriage per se,' Lalitha added.

'Even if I refuse, they will find another alliance if they are determined to marry you off.'

'I will take a call on that later. I want to complete my post-graduation and post-doctoral research to show myself what I am capable of.'

'You can still do that after marriage.' I liked this girl. She is very individualistic and knows her mind. Not a bad company for a wife.

I must keep my other ambitions at rest and settle on her. I always wanted to date a girl before I set about marrying. Take her around cafes and walks. Chat about families, ambitions, regrets, dreams, and even a smattering of films and cricket. I was willing to sacrifice all that fun for this girl who appeared to hold your gaze when you talked to her.

'Are you crazy? How can family commitments and career go hand in hand?'

'So many women have juggled family and profession successfully.'

'Let us not go there. You know our traditional family culture and the duties the daughter-in-law would have. Within the expectations of our big families, the dual responsibilities shall not work.'

'So, what do you want me to do?'

'Reject me. Say no on some pretext.'

'You can do that yourself too.'

'A lady can't do that in our society.' An annoyed tone.

He appeared to be a gentle, dedicated man with an unshakeable belief in the essential goodness of humanity. But the need to rage at him, to castigate him, rile against his acceptance of the proposal has consumed me.

My parents were pushing me to get married. They searched for alliances for me: right, left, and centre; sect no bar; groom should belong to Tamil Brahmin hierarchy. All because of that rascal, who made a spectacle of me in the street, watched by many onlookers. Having learnt the antecedents of that scoundrel's advocate father, my parents were worried about the repercussions of the FIR my Dad had lodged. That was when my paati raised the topic of the alliance with this young man living opposite our house.

My father, influenced by my paati, tried to convince me that Venkatraman would make a good life partner.

'Venkat graduated in Electrical Engineering from some college in Bengaluru. He then pursued a master's in Power Systems in North Carolina on scholarship and assistantship. I am not sure what made him return to Bengaluru after serving for a couple of years in the US. He presently works for a State Government Power Corporation and is in a senior position. His aunt lives with him. No one else shares their large house – ancestral property,' he said.

I noticed his compassion and found a true sense for the first time. I must be of value for such a man. But I have my career plans; anything else is secondary.

I saw a certain weariness burden Lalitha, and to my enormous dismay, she was greatly disturbed. She shook violently, paced the floor, and slumped on the sofa helplessly. I joined her and picked up her hand. I held it tightly, pressing it lovingly to assuage her fears. She smelled of fresh shampoo. She let me hold her hand. After a few minutes of complete silence – the only sound was of her heavy breathing and that of the rickety overhead fan – she pulled her hand from me and strutted out, closing the door behind her. Fortunately, attaih was away attending a Satsang, and no one was at home to witness the bitter encounter.

Later during the dinner, attaih told me that Sounder Rajan was in a hurry to find an alliance for his daughter, Lalitha. If necessary, beyond their sect too. And she went on extolling the virtues of his daughter. She was academically brilliant and an accomplished dancer too. She does all the household duties too. I was sure that the last quality was a bluff as they had two home-bound ladies who could well take care of homely tasks. Seriously, attaih!

An essential difference between Iyers and Iyengars is that while the Iyers believe in the supremacy of Lord Shiva, the Iyengars believe in the supremacy of Lord Vishnu. Iyengars are so strict that they don't perform any Shiva-related festivities like Ganesh Chaturthi or Mahashivaratri. Something serious could have forced the strictly religious Sounder, Rajan, to bury his sectorial differences to agree to find an alliance for his daughter with an Iyer. I needed not to go far to find the reason. Attaih provided the essence of the mystery.

Attaih could easily be a team member of Woodward and Bernstein.

* * *

The wishes of Lalitha's parents prevailed, despite Lalitha's protests. Also, after her talk with Venkat, Lalitha felt she could pursue her ambition of a career in science, even after marriage. So Lalitha reluctantly agreed to the marriage.

My marriage would keep the scoundrel away from me.

Venkatraman and Lalitha were married in an elaborate wedding ceremony, per the Tambrahm customs of Oonjal, Kashi yatra etc. Lalitha remembered an oft-repeated adage: a known devil is better than an unknown angel and settled for the wedding as it was inevitable. Also, Venkat appeared mild-mannered and could be manipulated to pursue her career ambitions.

A few of Venkat's friends, who could not attend the wedding, insisted on a party to formally introduce Lalitha. Socialising didn't appear to be on top of Lalitha's agenda. She reluctantly agreed. In the marriage, too, Venkat didn't notice any young ladies loitering near the bride wearing exotic outfits giggling and joking, a phenomenon one usually would find in any wedding. Lalitha didn't have a friend circle to boast of.

She was at the dressing table in a yellow silk saree with a red border and mango icons. Venkat felt protective of her and quietly went around, grabbed her from behind, and kissed her neck.

She turned around and said, 'What was that for?'

'Nothing,' he replied, 'Just felt like kissing you.'

Ignoring that comment, she said, 'Is there anyone at the party I need to watch out for?'

'None whatsoever. If it is so required, I shall point it out to you.'

That was the last party that Venkat and Lalitha attended during their lifetime.

Sex with Lalitha had been calmer than Venkat anticipated. He did not overdo the physical intimacy and waited for her to build trust in him. He thought it would help her feel safe and secure with a man who appeared in her life from nowhere and under strange circumstances. Venkat thought that things might start to develop into something more exciting. For the first month, sex had been an afterthought with Lalitha that they did at the end of every night as a ritual than any passionate lovemaking.

As time rolled by, Venkat felt bored. Bored of soft thrusting, gentle caressing and final ejaculation.

It turned worse once she was found to be pregnant.

Chapter 4

I was reassured by seeing no change on the dipstick, even though I missed my regular period, which was very unusual. My menstrual bleeding timing is as regimental as I was – exactly after 28 days. I did not take it easy.

My family doctor assured me it was normal to have a delayed period after losing one's virginity.

'With the first intercourse itself, your hormones get active, and there are chances your period may get delayed. Fret not; this is not a pregnancy alarm, but rather your body telling you it's going through changes. It is not necessarily a reason to doubt any pregnancy. Let us wait ten more days and redo the tests,' the doctor said.

When I said that I could not concentrate on my academic work, the doctor said, 'This is due to the hormonal changes and can make you feel extremes of emotions, affecting your concentration. Don't worry, child. It is normal. After a few more unions, it will be normal, and you will feel happy.'

Venkatraman was a bit upset when I told him I had missed my period.

He was too anxious to consummate the marriage; he did not broach the protection topic. I succumbed too. So foolish of me.

'Lalitha, about the first night. I had not used any protection, and I am now worried. Sorry, we should have discussed this before. Everything happened so fast that there was no privacy time for us to discuss our future life.'

'I told you not to worry,' I said confidently, based on the doctor's assurance.

'I am worried. I need to know if there is a chance of pregnancy.'

'No,' I said quickly and hoped to Ganesha it was true.

'You know for sure?' I nodded.

After ten days, I did a retest as recommended by my gynaecologist.

I let my breath go in a long exhalation as I looked at myself in the mirror. I wouldn't be pregnant, I told herself. All my plans would go kaput. We had sex on all three days; the elders had given us as per tradition. No big deal. Sure, he hadn't used any protection for the first day. He apologised for the indiscretion and used a condom for the next three days. I was a willing partner too.

I thought that a single penetration without protection should not matter as many friends of mine got away with it all the time when in a passionate embrace, they had spontaneous intercourse.

* * *

I became busy with my academic schedules, and Venkat had gone to Raipur on some Project work. During the retest, I carefully followed the instructions for the self-test as instructed by my gynaecologist. *I will be okay... I will be okay*, I assured myself. The indicator turned negative. But the delayed periods were giving me the creeps.

This time I took my mom to see the doctor.

She checked whether I took the test on the first urination of the morning without drinking water. I said yes.

'You can be pregnant even with a negative indication as the HCG hormone levels are too low to be detected by the test,' she said.

'If you're pregnant but aren't aware of it, missing pregnancy symptoms can add to the confusion. Especially if you've never been pregnant before, it's easy to dismiss pregnancy symptoms such as fatigue as the result of dietary or lifestyle choices,' she added.

Then she ordered for Ultrasound test to recheck.

To my dismay, the doctor confirmed that I was pregnant and the foetus was healthy.

Is it possible to conceive at the first attempt itself? Well, I proved it. I can sympathise with rape victims who become mothers, much to their annoyance.

But I was determined to complete my post-graduation course and regularly attended the classes and corresponding labs. One evening I was about to leave the college; I felt dizzy with blurred vision and could not walk on a straight path. My classmate, Vara, noticed this, immediately called for an auto, and took me home.

My mom rushed me to the hospital on the telephone recommendation of our family doctor.

After some tests and scans, without explaining any medical reasoning, the hospital gynaecologist – an elderly gentleman, insisted that I should have bed rest entirely and could not move out alone. They recommended hospitalisation to ensure complete bed rest and close monitoring of both the foetus and the mother. On my insistence, my mom assured the doctors that whatever was required to ensure safe delivery would be guaranteed in her home care with a full-time nurse if needed. So that put an end to my further progress in academics.

I wanted to cry. A lot. My mother wanted me to shift to my ancestral house, but I refused. I assured her that Venkat's Attaih was quite efficient and kind and would take care of me.

Venkat returned from his tour and was apologetic, reassuring Lalitha that once the baby was delivered, she could go back to finish her planned academic goals. When Venkat heard the confirmation of conception, the thought of procreation excited him enormously. He hoped Lalitha, too, would feel the same way. But he was disappointed by her violent reaction. Yet afterwards, when they counted, they were certain that she conceived on the first night. Lalitha cursed him for not using protection. 'You know you've been a complete and utter fool.'

Her mother came to Venkat's rescue. She told her that conception at the early stage of marriage was good as, in the later years, the mother could be free to accept any career. This assurance calmed Lalitha a bit.

'We will be losing just one year. We have our Attaih to look after the child, and we can also have some hired help.'

I had to agree because aborting the foetus was not an option I was willing to accept, even though it was just ten weeks old. If God wanted me to be a mother, so be it. My mom wanted me to shift to her house, which I refused. I was determined to make changes to my husband's home to make it a livable entity with modern amenities when my baby arrived.

* * *

'We must sell this house and buy or construct a new one,' Lalitha announced

'We have been living in Malleshwaram for the past 80 years. Of course, the colony is a little overcrowded now, but the market is nearby, and so are schools, colleges, temples and hospitals,' said Venkat.

'I don't want to live in the same colony as that scoundrel who messed up my life.'

That was not the only reason why Lalitha wanted to relocate.

This house has an ancient look. It's mouldy. I don't want my child to be raised in this house.

When Lalitha went to Venkat's home, she found brown water stains spreading on the walls, sofa covers scuffed and torn, and many such objects long past their deadline for repairs. Very untidy house. Very unbecoming of a Brahmin home. His aunt was too old to look after the house and make it habitable per modern standards. A woman with a contemporary outlook is needed for the proper upkeep of a place to make it a home. Lalitha set about a total overhaul of the house, which even the perennially cynical aunt appreciated.

She instructed Venkat often on how to keep the home neat and tidy, not to dirty the front room with his shoes and such trivialities.

Lalitha made sure that the house was run like a tight ship. You can't walk around in a towel. Flush the toilet such that all evidence of any previous visit is removed. You can't walk into the house with footwear from outside. You can have slippers inside the house, though. But they are not to be taken out of the home. If you are in a hurry and did take them out, they must be soap-washed before reusing them at home. Television should not be loud—that annoyed Attaih, who was hard of hearing. A week into her stay in his home, Venkat found many rules to remember.

Whatever renovations she tried, the house was too old to bear the constant battering by the workers. One day she found a wall had a crack, the result of the carpenter's hammer.

That was the ultimate proverbial nail.

Venkat thought Lalitha was mad to consider relocating to a new house but eventually gave way to her reasoning.

They argued on and on. About probable locations. About finances. Prebuilt or to be constructed as per own design. Independent house or apartment. And the like. With no consensus.

But Lalitha was not the one to give up. She searched and searched. She contacted many house brokers. She found that a new colony beyond Hebbal, north of Bengaluru, was coming up with all amenities – specially reserved for government employees, with some conditions.

Sahakaranagara was formed by the Ministry of Communication Employees housing society and has developed to a large extent under the efforts of the Sahakaranagara Residents Welfare Association. The association was forced to extend the society membership to include local State Government employees, too, as they needed local help for water, electricity other municipal ward connectivity.

She found that Venkat's position in the State Government allowed him to fulfil the changed criterion for buying a plot.

From then on, Lalitha worked as a woman possessed and could find an open plot of one thousand square yards on the 8th Main for an affordable sum. By now, the bulge on her body was showing. She was six months pregnant. Early pregnancy discomfiture was reduced to a large extent. But travelling was still a pain, with public transport facilities not conducive to comfort, availability and affordability. She went into early labour when the plot was allotted and readied for construction.

Lalitha was rushed to the hospital. Doctor Smita Vartak, a well-known gynaecologist at Aster Hospital, said after examining her, 'Stress could be a reason for the false labour pains.'

Smita Vartak is a practising Obstetrician & Gynaecologist with an experience of over 15 years. She is an esteemed member of the Bangalore Society of Obstetrics & Gynaecology, Federation of Obstetric and Gynaecological Societies of India (FOGSI), and Royal College of Obstetricians & Gynaecologists, London.

Pavitra complained, 'She is overexerting lately in trying to shift her residence. She travels across the city to find a new home for her. I wanted to warn her, but she did not listen.

The doctor turned to Lalitha and addressed her. 'We have noticed an increase in cortisol, epinephrine and norepinephrine levels. Overexertion surely is the cause. Overtaxing your body could cause your uterus to start "false" contractions. If you're doing too much work, you could cause Braxton Hicks contractions.'

Smita warned her and recommended hospitalisation for continuous monitoring and preventive actions.

Smita hinted that she wanted to talk privately with Lalitha's mother.

'Does she have a peaceful family life?'

'There is no reason to doubt that. My son-in-law is a good person. But as you know, what happens between the husband and wife within the four walls of their bedroom, only God knows.'

'The foetus is almost 34 weeks old and appears weak in the Ultrasound. Is she getting good nutrition?'

'I have no knowledge of that except what she confides in me. She is staying at her in-laws' place only. So I have no first-hand knowledge.'

'That is unusual. For the first child delivery, the woman typically shifts to her parent's house as early as the 20th week because she needs good care and motherly advice and love. Not that it may not be available in the in-law's place. Yet, that is the practice established by our tradition, which has a scientific bearing.'

'Yes, of course, but she refused to shift her residence despite our repeated requests.'

Smita shrugged and said, 'Full term is 39-40 weeks. Anything less than that is premature. I fear FGR. Fetal growth restriction (FGR) is a condition in which an unborn baby (fetus) is smaller than expected for the number of weeks of pregnancy (gestational age). It is often described as an estimated weight less than the 10th percentile. Regular and early prenatal care, a healthy diet, and steady weight gain help to prevent FGR and other problems. That is why I have recommended hospital monitoring.'

Within a few weeks of admittance, Lalitha broke water. The doctors rushed her to the delivery room, and a senior gynaecologist asked to be present as this was a preterm delivery and needed close supervision. Lalitha's parents were also summoned in case of emergency surgical intervention. Venkat was also rushed from his office as directed by attaih. Ultrasound measurements indicated that the fetus was only 16'' long against the 18-20'' norm. The labour room team had to adapt to C-section delivery. The baby needed to be admitted to a neonatal intensive care unit (NICU) because her weight was 2.5 kgs, much below the average.

Sounder Rajan contacted Dr Smita Vartak, who came rushing to the hospital. She assured all the family members that such deliveries were not unusual and that they need not panic.

'You are in good hands, and we shall ensure that both the mother and the child are taken care of. Last year 73 per cent of babies were born before their due dates. Only 1% of babies did not survive. All those who did not survive were in rural India, where medical facilities are non-existent for such emergencies.'

Venkat was surprised to notice the change in Lalitha's attitude. In the maternity ward, Lalitha was lying with her head resting against her pillow. Her face strained with tough delivery. Fortunately, the baby was healthy. Lalitha was holding the baby very delicately. What all happened within the last nine and half months between them seemed to have dissolved as she saw the baby now clinging to her breast. She was yelling furiously as she was unable to suck. The nurse came and helped to adjust the baby to feel comfortable. Lalitha thanked her and caressed the head of the baby as she now started suckling. What change can motherhood bring in a lady?

It took over three years of intensive care in hospitals and at home for Kaveri to be an average child. That put paid to Lalitha's dream of a career in science.

* * *

Lalitha carried the bag of groceries into the kitchen and dumped them on the table. She pulled item by item and placed them in order of the eventual storage compartment of the fridge. *This is what marriage has done to me. The highlight of the day is the arrival of shopping items.*

Lalitha never stopped wondering how she got trapped into this matrimony and motherhood, abandoning all her ambitions of pursuing a research career in Solid State Physics.

Miraculously Kaveri became a bright young girl growing up to four years old. Pavitra said her grandchild was very much a replica of a young Lalitha. Lalitha spent most of her waking time tending to her daughter. Though it did disappoint her that she could not pursue her goals, she took pride in nurturing her daughter, now lovingly called by her pet name, Ponni.

After realising that she no longer can continue her original ambition, she decided to take up her other favourite goal – dancing. But there was a gap of four years in her dancing practices because of marriage and complications during delivery, and her child also needed constant care.

Lalitha was not the one to give up. She went to Chennai and enrolled in the popular Vempati Chinna Satyam's dance academy to upskill. As Kaveri was still young, Lalitha took her child along while she stayed in the hostel of the dance schools. This was much resented by Venkat's attaih. However, Venkat supported Lalitha as he felt he was partly responsible for the loss of her first passion for scientific research. She continued her retraining in Bharatanatyam from Kalindhi Narayanan and learnt Abhinaya from her.

When Kaveri was toilet trained and could begin schooling, Lalitha started teaching dance to young children at hired premises in Sahakaranagara.

PART 2

TWO DECADES LATER

Chapter 5

Fifteen years on, the house Lalitha built at Sahakaranagar looked as she had planned. There was a sturdy gate for the car to drive into the garage and a wicket gate for pedestrians. A stone path and rose bushes on either side lead you to the front door. The walls were full of creepers of all types, which presented a pleasant scenario. Red, White and Pink hibiscus plants strategically mingled with marigold and lily plants are visible all around the house. She emphasised the need for a kitchen garden and sowed daily needs of coriander, curry leaf, eggplant and the like. She took care of the foliage by hiring a part-time gardener for advice and de-weeding.

Despite her busy schedule at the dance school, she made cooking look simple and inviting. While she was cooking, the aroma of the masalas permeated the house. Yet, she would place the cooked food on the table without bothering to serve it. Venkat helped himself. They mostly ate in silence. Though Venkat never stopped appreciating her culinary skills while enjoying the food, she would nod and say something unconnected to the food. 'Tonight, I may come late; one of my students is having a party.' Kind of.

She refused to accept his passionate plea to continue their marital relations as a normal couple. She denied him conjugal bliss on the pretext of her doctor's advice of rest and no vigorous activity. After her delivery also, she never gave in to him. 'There is plenty of time in our lives; let us wait,' was her constant refrain.

Venkat lived his life as a married bachelor. He cursed his luck and immersed himself in his job. Never did he force himself on her. Whether she acknowledged his gentlemanliness was not apparent. However, she had performed other wifely duties with élan. On his part, too, he had allowed as much freedom as a good husband would give his wife. Venkat let her choose her dance career and supported her by providing the infrastructural space for her dance school.

She had refused his hints to have sex. His attempts of caressing her breasts and thighs, hoping that the woman in her got aroused – had been of no use. She would brush away his hand and move away from him.

Sometimes she looked more like a stranger to him than his wife. Venkat felt that he had lost all his sexual appetite. He wanted to prove that he could get it up once to demonstrate his virility. But looking at her, Venkat felt nothing. Suddenly he wanted her to get out of sight, so he could suppress his thoughts and concentrate on his work. When the sexual urge consumed him, he would drum gibberish on his desktop computer out of anger, not at her, but at his misfortune.

Does Mangamma know about the fissures in our relationship? While changing the duvets, she must have noticed our queen-size beds are one foot apart. She works in a couple of other houses too. I wonder if she gossips! When Ponni was young, we requested the maid to take on only one more job as we needed her for a longer time, especially when Ponni returned from school in the evening. But now she works in three more houses.

A few times, Venkat imagined making love to Lalitha in the shower – drops trickling over her breasts as he licked away the drops arousing her. And made love to her in the bath – doggy position with the water dripping on her back as he moved in and out. The fictional experience remained in the realm of his aspirations.

Venkat and Lalitha seemed to have less and less rapport nowadays. He wondered if Lalitha had sensed the gap growing exponentially between them. Though, there was no open hostility. Lalitha, with her calm nature, would not let that happen. Composed and competent, she made a perfect housemaker. With the good looks she possessed, this character made her more pretty. Venkat never ceased to respect Lalitha as a housemaker and mother. It was simply his marriage that had become uninteresting, even dull. Lalitha found solace in dance after losing hope in pursuing her passion for scientific research; she immersed herself in her dance school. Venkat's job pressure had put a strain on his time at home, resulting in a monosyllable talk with Lalitha. So many nights, he came home late from work, after Lalitha had gone to bed, and collapsed on the living room sofa, exhausted. And so many mornings, he left for work in the early dark for site visits.

Venkat often found Lalitha to be meticulous, regimental and unpredictable. Despite her busy dance schedule, she never neglected Kaveri. She took care of her academic calendar and ensured all the infrastructure needed for Kaveri to excel. Lalitha wished that Kaveri would pursue her education to become a researcher in any field she chooses and earn a doctoral qualification, which she sorely missed. Lalitha wanted to see herself in Kaveri. Sounder Rajan, Lalitha's father, had always found Ponni a replica of Lalitha. Not in looks alone. 'Mark my words; she will be a bright girl.' He remembered that he had said the same about Lalitha too.

Kaveri, an optimistic child, pretended not to notice the silent treatment her parents were giving to each other. She was convinced that if she worked hard in her academics and behaved well, whatever it was that made their parents unhappy would blow over.

Kaveri always wondered what a perfect marriage would look like.

The couple understood each other; each gave way about issues that didn't matter and talked their way through that which did. The loving couple would bring a new dimension into each other lives: honesty and trust.

Kaveri hoped she would find one such partner.

* * *

Lalitha's dance academy had run into problems with the local corporator. He insisted on bribe money to prevent the ward officer in cahoots with the local police from objecting to the parking of cycles and scooters at the entrance gate of her dance school premises. The haphazard parking did not affect the traffic flow, but it presented a chaotic image. Venkat had no time to settle the matter. Meanwhile, police took away a couple of cycles of the girls, which annoyed their parents. The neighbours were uncooperative; it seemed one of them had tipped off the police.

Lalitha managed the matter with the help of the landlord, who had allowed a portion of her garden to be converted into a parking place. Yet the site was not sufficient for all the students. Lalitha had to readjust her class timings and started taking classes in shifts. She was upset that Venkat did not help her solve the matter. She was distraught because Venkat had promised her one life and given her another. At every stage of her adolescent life, she ran into complications. First, the stalker, then the reluctant marriage, then the pregnancy and related complications and forced abandonment of her post-grad course. Finally, Lalitha settled into routine married life, each pursuing their career or passion. It rankled her. However, Lalitha's dance institute became popular, and many of her students also went on to give public performances that their parents and the audience appreciated.

That was when the Indian diaspora in the USA was wooed by Indian musicians, yoga experts, Indologists, and dancers to learn about Indian culture. Lalitha's college-mate Vara, who married a doctor in Atlanta, visited her to revive an old acquaintance. Knowing about Lalitha's dance school, she proposed the idea of Lalitha's performance in the upcoming Indian Cultural Festival organised by the US Kannada Association in Atlanta. Kaveri had already grown and was pursuing a college education, and Lalitha was free to travel. Venkat gave consent and arranged all the required formalities of visa, ticketing and the like.

Lalitha's performance was a hit, and many parents approached her to teach dance to their children. Also, one of Vara's friends who worked at UNESCO invited Lalitha to perform at an Asian festival in Paris. Her image as an excellent Indian dance teacher had spread across the US and Europe. During the US summertime, Lalitha was invited by NRIs to train their children. She would spend every July to September conducting dance workshops across North America.

She became a sought-after teacher in the US. She performed many arangentrams[1] in various cities of the USA – Chicago, Dallas, Washington DC, and Maryland - to name a few.

Meanwhile, Kaveri came of age and became an Electronics Engineer. During her campus interview, she got selected by a Baltimore-based company with a branch in Bengaluru. Last summer, mother and daughter travelled together to the US – Kaveri for training and Lalitha to continue her dance assignments.

---

1. Arangetram is the debut on-stage performance of the Indian dance "Bharatanatyam" student

Chapter 6

As I entered the Chairman's chambers, I saw our MD, CE and two other gentlemen seated.

'Hello, Mr Subramanian, please be seated,' said the Chairman, Gopala Krishna Goud, of Bengaluru Power Corporation.

I have been working with State Power Utilities since I returned from the US after gaining a few years of experience in the Public Utility sector in California and Arizona.

'Venkatraman, sir,' I corrected.

Tamil names are different from those of other compatriots. We write our father's name first and our given name at the end. Generally, people confuse the name that appears first as our first name and address us as such. I had to do these corrections often.

'Yes, I am sorry, Venkatraman. You know our Managing Director and Chief Engineer (projects), the person on your right is the secretary of the Minister for Power of the State.'

Bengaluru Power Corporation was recently carved out of the State Power and Transmission Corporation to ensure special care to the booming IT sector in the town.

The Chairpersons of corporations are not appointed on merit or any other appraisal system but by nomination by the party in power. When there is a change in the government administration, these chairpersons change accordingly to the whims of the ruling politicians.

Primarily the appointees are drawn from the elected representatives of the party in power. As all the legislative members can't be made to cabinet, some are accommodated as chairperson posts – just decorative. In rare instances, a prominent public figure is also made a chairperson to acknowledge the person's contribution to the party in power or the government.

He did not introduce the other person. Later I was to learn that he was the son of the minister.

'We are here to discuss the Thimmalahalli 33kv/11kv substation tender.' That was my MD, Sethuramaiah.

'Our study had shown that most of the tenders were being awarded to the same limited group of contractors as though they were in a cartel. In our meeting a few months back, we decided that the Board has to find a way to award this tender to the new contractor so that we have more competition.' *Very noble thought indeed.*

'True, sir. We make the qualification criterion per the norms of the Board's technical committee and CVC guidelines. However, as recommended by the tender committee, we had tweaked the PQC[2] requirement experience limit to 11Kv and the previous contracts completed from 5 to 2, and substantially toned down the financial criterion allowing smaller firms to compete. We have also added a clause wherein the bidder could take up the previous contracts through subcontract. – i.e. need not be directly from a State or Central government. The lowest tender with all these criteria came from one Sri Venkateshwar Designers and Contractors, also first-time entrants to our Board. Thus the finance department, upon the tender committee's recommendation, has told us to award the contract to Sri Venkateshwar. This decision also fulfils our need to increase the participating tenderers in future.'

2. Pre-qualification Criterion

As he moved forward in his chair, the Chairman appeared disappointed by this appraisal. He turned to the MD and addressed him, ignoring me.

'You know the minister wants to build a paved road in his village connecting to the new highway coming up. This new road would help the villagers to take their produce to the main market in the town nearby. The panchayat does not have the finance. The State Road department cannot help as they are cash-starved, have exceeded their budget allocation and many contractors are already upset with the department for late payments. The minister had approached me to help. I convinced an electrical contractor, Bhogam Electricians, to bid for this tender as the owner promised to use the profit from this contract to build the road to help the minister for a future quid-pro-quo. But I am told that he came second lowest, not the lowest. You have to help me somehow and award the contract to Bhogam. I don't know how you do it. But do it.'

Now I understand why the tender qualification criterion was diluted, not for the altruistic motive of bringing in more competition but for helping the minister. I learned later that Bhogam Electricians is owned by the minister's son's friend and a benami[3] *unit of the minister's family.*

'Rest assured, sir. We shall find a solution,' said the MD.

MD instructed me to hold the letter of intent.

A letter of Intent is the first step in executing the contract when the winning bidder is asked to mobilise resources and start work. The

---

3. 'Benami' in Hindi translates to 'no name' or 'without a name. A Benami business would be one where a person's name is not used, but the name of another person or a fictitious person is used instead.

final agreement would follow in due course – which generally takes a month more. LOI is a way to speed up the execution process to save time in preparing the legal formalities of the contract documentation.

The meeting was then dispersed.

After a few days, Sethuramaiah called for a meeting with Finance, me, and my tech team. He asked for a few details from Finance on the winning bidder's financial capability and then addressed the gathering.

'I have also made some inquiries with my sources about this L1 contractor, Sri Venkateshwar Designers and Contractors. He was awarded two contracts of similar nature – one from the Andhra Pradesh Electricity Board and another from Bokaro Steel Plant (BSP) through MECON. The BSP contract is not yet completed for nearly five years, though the agreed completion schedule was for two years. The contractor filed a lawsuit against BSP and MECON and abandoned the works mid-way. We have a clause in our general terms and conditions that if the contractor gives false information, he can be barred. I believe the contractor has produced documents about the award of the Contract from BSP but not the completion, also not been transparent on the litigation. I am unsure if we give the contract to this bidder; the contractor may not finish the contract in the stipulated time, which is the essence of our contract. Please consider how we can disqualify the lowest tenderer and award the Contract to Bhogam without violating any CVC and Board guidelines. In a hurry to please the Minister or me, please do not put the Chairman or me in problems.'

'Sir, we need proof of such litigation details and documents from BSP or MECON to put on record. We can't work on hearsay,' said our CE.

'I am aware of that. I have a copy of the letter written by Bokaro to this contractor with me and made a few copies to be given to you. Let me read the vital part of this letter:

'You have withdrawn your personnel from the site without informing us. You are required to mobilise the resources within fifteen days, failing which suitable action shall be initiated.'

I hope this is enough for you to disqualify this tenderer,' said Sethuramaiah.

'Sir, this letter is dated about four months back,' I said, 'we don't have any documented information on the present status.'

'I am sure your staff is competent to get the latest information and finalise the action in consultation with the Tender committee. I have given my input. The work needs to be done within one month from today. Please take it as the final target. Beyond which I will take action as I deem fit.'

Sethuramaiah walked out of the conference room without formally closing the meeting. What I was being instructed to do was not the kind of thing I am good at handling.

CE looked at me and shrugged, and he also walked out. The ball was very much in my court now.

The Finance manager, Ambrish Varma, came to my rescue and said he knew some people in MECON's Bengaluru office from whom he might get some inside information on the contract. Since my appointment at the Elec Board eleven years ago, the finance manager and I had shared a mutual liking and habitually confided in each other. From time to time, I had taken many a favour from him to help a few distressed contractors whose work got held up because of delayed payments preventing them from paying the wages to their sub-vendors and sub-contractors.

Mr Varma took the letter copy that Sethuramaiah had given us and returned to his chambers.

* * *

I decided to do something I had not done before – talk to a bidder before the contract award.

I asked my assistant to fix an appointment with the owner of Sri Venkateshwar Designers and Contractors.

Raman Rao is a qualified electrical engineer who worked in Power Grid, Delhi, before venturing independently. He has been in the contracting business for the past seven years.

When my staff contacted him, the receptionist said that Raman Rao was about to leave for Delhi for a meeting and that he could come to our Board's office if it were urgent. I did not want anyone from my office to notice me talking to Raman Rao. I told my staff to fix a time to meet him at his house before his departure to wherever he was going. It was arranged, and I met Raman Rao at the appointed hour.

I crammed myself into Maruti Zen, provided by Varma. My vehicle was to be upgraded commensurate to my elevation to Superintending Engineer. It was taking time because of bureaucratic hurdles. I headed towards Sanjay Nagar, a posh residential colony of Bengaluru. As it was mid-afternoon, there was not much traffic, and I could drive quickly. I found a parking spot to avoid traffic challan and walked up to the house.

The door was opened by a young man who led me to a large hall as soon as I announced my name and designation. The room was functional, fully used, and had no space wastage. There were neatly filled cabinets lined with books of various genres. Floor-ceiling glass partitions in place of a wall overlooked a balcony. I was surprised to notice a contractor with such highly evolved tastes. My impression of contractors was that they have the bare minimum academic achievements, and business is mainly passed from generation to generation by acquiring wealth by dubious means.

A man, medium build, wheatish complexioned, wearing rimless glasses, walked from an adjoining room after fifteen minutes. I shook hands and introduced myself. Felt his grip was firm. Confidence. He had a hardy determination that seemed to ooze from his demeanour. Of course, the world of Government contracting is not done on a level playing field. You have to be ruthless and cunning, at the same time, appear professional when required.

'Please excuse my bad manners. Keeping you waiting for so long. The tele-talk took longer than I anticipated. Sorry, we did not even offer you a chair,' Raman Rao apologetically led me to a sofa set with two single-seater and one large three-seater. All in ash grey colour tapestry covered. I chose the single-seater. He faced me on another single-seater.

'I don't believe we have met,' he said, 'you could have asked me to come to your office. Why did you take this trouble?'

I introduced myself and said, 'I did not want my office staff to see you in my office. The purpose of our meeting is very confidential.'

'Ok. Tell me, sir, what can I do for you?'

I explained the predicament I was in, giving the gist of the Minister's interest in the contract, ostensibly for an altruistic motive. However, neither he nor I believed it was the valid reason for the Minister's interest in the contract.

'I *am* feeling like Dornacharya demanding the thumb of ekalvya,' I added ruefully.

'I still don't understand what you want from me.'

'Firstly, please explain to me the issue you have with the Bokaro Steel contract, which is being taken as a ruse to disqualify you so that the tender is awarded to the second lowest.'

Then he explained at length.

'My firm, Sri Venkateshwar Designers and Contractors (SVDC), was awarded the contract by Bokaro Steel Plant (BSP) for power supply to their sinter plant under construction as a part of their expansion plan. MECON were their consultant. MECON is a Ranchi-based consultancy organisation with a branch office in Bengaluru. All civil works of foundations were the in the scope of BSP. SVDC were responsible for the electrical part of the job. MECON regularly delayed the approval of drawings, delayed inspections, delayed site clearance for work progress, and delayed dispatch instructions. These delays had added to our costs as we had to wait forever for these approvals. Our staff had to stay put at the site for these clearances, twiddling thumbs for days on end, sometimes months too. When I complained to BSP's Contract Manager, he shrugged and said, "we have to learn to manage these things in a government contract." From the BSP side, their civil work scope was also delayed beyond the scheduled PERT chart we had jointly prepared. For instance, for the tile flooring of 500sft, their civil contractor took three months to complete that, too, not as per agreed specs, and all the time, my staff had to wait at the site idling.

After constantly following up and being exasperated with all avenues of resolution, I withdrew my engineers and staff from the site. On top of all this, they deducted our milestone payments for late delivery for no fault. Instead of helping us resolve the issues with MECON, BSP managers washed their hands off and informed us that they shall settle all the payment deductions at the time of the last bill payment. Deducting ten per cent from every running bill means that my company was simply working on a no-profit basis. I could not go on like this forever. So I filed a lawsuit after receiving the letter from BSP to restart the work by redeploying our staff and equipment to the site, giving me a deadline,' Raman Rao said.

'Our department is trying to disqualify you based on your litigant nature as evidenced by the suit you have filed against BSP and MECON.'

'That is unfair. My complaint is genuine. I have filed the suit after failing to get a fair hearing in the arbitration meeting. Further, the statement in the arbitration clause – the contractor should not stop the work during the arbitration proceedings – riled us. This clause is against the principle of fair play. That is what forced me to go to court.'

'I understand. If our Board disqualifies you on the ground that you are a perennial litigant, you can go to the court of law on the ground that you are being victimised. You can also ask for a stay on the tender finalisation till the court decides one way or the other.'

'I cannot understand whether you are arguing for the government or me,' Raman Rao wondered.

'I am on the side of development. As you know, this substation is very important for the government as it feeds the proposed Japanese Investment coming up in a couple of years, which will boost our industrial sector by helping ancillaries and giving employment opportunities. Any foolish act by my seniors would have repercussions beyond one simple contract. I have to find a way that our tender committee doesn't act foolishly that may force you to take the legal course as explained earlier, which will substantially delay the power connectivity deadline given by the Centre to us.'

'I still need clarification on what you want from me.'

'Simple. Please help me find a loophole in your bid so we can legally cancel your bid. I can find the same with the help of my staff, but it will take time. Time is one thing we don't have. As you are the one who filled the tender, you would know where you have missed on a clause or a requirement,' I said.

'This is preposterous. You want me to cut my hand. This tender is important for me too. I have deliberately filed a low bid, on which I shall incur a loss. I want to showcase this work as a part of our company's achievement and growth. In no way can I agree to your request.'

I could notice slight irritation in his tone.

'I am only trying to invoke your patriotic spirit. My Board may take a foolish step by disqualifying you on some flimsy ground to satisfy a Minister's whim which can't stand legal scrutiny, and the collateral damage would be huge.'

That was my Brahmastra[4]

'Presumably, say you invoked my patriotic spirit, and I don't take further steps in signing the contract. I will not only lose this opportunity to add to my eligibility criterion for future tenders, but I could also be blacklisted, and my EMD of ten lakhs shall be forfeited.'

'I may have a solution for all your apprehensions. Just say yes, and I will do the rest. Regarding the EMD, we shall work it out after talking with my Finance department. I shall also recommend the Chairman and our MD about your generosity and will ensure future tender help and works in the Board.'

---

4. A missile set by divine forces – a weapon with insurmountable capabilities

'I am not with you on this. Anyway, I need to consult my investors and staff before deciding. Please give me a couple of days. I will return to Bengaluru on Monday and will contact you then.'

We bid goodbye, and I left.

During the drive back to my office, I realised I didn't have lunch. Once the unopened lunch box gets home, Lalitha will give a sermon on how taking timely meals is essential for good health.

* * *

Back in my office, I am far from any solution than when I left to meet Raman Rao. After an hour of checking emails and signing off a few documents, I walked into Ambrish's room at the far end of the building. He was seriously studying a thick book, the title of which I could not read. He put a bookmark in and signalled me to sit.

'Coffee?'

'Yeah, some snacks also; I did not have lunch.'

I briefed him about my meeting with L1 and how I failed to persuade him to find a way to withdraw his tender.

'I can suggest a solution if EMD[5] is the only problem. Regarding giving Raman Rao another chance, you know we have the Gauribidnur tender due next month. We can accommodate him in that bid.'

---

5. Earnest Money Deposit: this is a deposit to ensure that the bidder stands by the clauses of the tender if his tender is accepted. EMD, as such, is a guarantee to ensure that rouge firms don't make a mockery of the tender process

Ambrish Varma is a brilliant chartered accountant. He passed his CA qualification tests when he was hardly twenty-two, which was a record of sorts. And above all, he is well-read on all legal and financial aspects and up-to-date on all judgements and rulings of all courts concerning contract laws. Everyone, including the MD, seeks his advice on personal income tax matters. The tender committee values his comments and remarks on any tender validations.

Then he went on explaining to me a recent Karnataka High Court order on EMD[6]

'In a writ petition by a contractor of BRUHAT BENGALURU MAHANAGARA PALIKE,

WRIT PETITION NO.14154, the contractor who was L1, said that he did not receive any notification or letter from BBMP to sign the agreement to execute the contract during the offer validity of 90 days. As the BBMP had not chosen to call upon the petitioner to execute the deal during the validity period, the contractor withdrew his tender and asked for the return of the EMD. The BBMP refused, citing a clause wherein it was said that if the contractor withdrew his offer, he would forfeit his EMD. But the court noticed that BBMP approached the contractor for negotiations after the expiry of the offer's validity. Hence, the contractor is at liberty to withdraw the offer and is entitled to the refund of EMD.'

'As you know, we have reduced the validity from the normal 90 days to 60 days in this tender as we wanted to put pressure on the tender committee to finalise the contract evaluation quickly so that the work can start, as it was a time-bound project,' added Varma.

6.

'Thank you, Ambrish, you have taken off a big botheration from me. Let's call for a meeting of the Tender committee and our MD to decide on the further course of action.'

I soon finished my day's work and started back home. It was late; my driver Subbaih was not around and, on inquiry, was told that he had given the car key to security and had to leave home because of an emergency. I perforce had to self-drive the vehicle.

While driving, my attention went home. I started thinking about Lalitha as I drove along.

I noticed that Lalitha would be upset that I am not maintaining meal timings and missing them for one reason or another.

I reached home and parked my newly allotted Toyota SUV near the side entrance on the footpath of the road, as Lalitha's Santro occupied the garage. I walked in and found Lalitha on the sofa staring at the TV images on mute.

'You get freshened up. I will make fresh dosas for you,' Lalitha said while turning off the TV.

'Ok. Has Kaveri finished her dinner?'

'Yes, she had and is upstairs working or reading. I don't know.'

After dinner, I retired to bed wondering how to approach the tender committee to convince them of what Ambrish had suggested.

Chapter 7

It took one more week to assemble all the members of the Tender Committee, along with CE and MD.

'So, what is the plan, Venkatraman?' asks Sethuramaiah, the Managing Director.

I explain the details with Ambrish Varma chipping in.

'Do you think L1 will agree to withdraw?' asks CE Parthasarathy.

'There is another issue we have to deal with before we invite L1 for discussions,' says Ambrish before I could reply.

'What is that?' asks Sethuramaiah

'We can award the contract to L2 only if the bidder matches the price quoted by L1 as per CVC guidelines.'

I was not aware of this. Ambrish did not disclose this aspect when I met him. But now I see that the CE and the MD are a bit taken aback.

'What is the difference in price?' asks Sethuramaiah.

'About 6%.' I chip in.

'If he doesn't?'

'Then we have to re-tender.'

'Out of the question. We shall lose precious time, and the Central Government will come heavy on us,' says Sethuramaiah.

Behind this exchange, there is a background.

The contract for the construction of the substation is to ensure quality power to a Toshiba-Mitsubishi semi-conductor manufacturing unit expected to be commissioned within the next eighteen months. Japanese are well-known for conforming to schedules. Hence our work has to start and finish in the next twelve months—the Minister's directive of contract award to Bhogam notwithstanding. We are now in a fix. The difference in the price of L1 and L2 is significant, and even if Bhogam matches the price, there may not be enough surplus to help the Minister.

When I mention these apprehensions, the CE says, 'Let us not be presumptuous. We shall tackle the matter with separate teams. Venkat shall handle the L1 end, and a team comprising of Ambrish and I shall talk to Niranjan Agnihotri of Bhogam constructions.'

The meeting ends with a promise to meet again after a couple of days.

On Monday, I call up Raman Rao for a meeting. He agrees to meet at Taj near Trinity circle.

While entering the hotel lounge, I noticed Raman Rao having animated conversations with a middle-aged lady. He introduces her as Bhruha Kandala, his Accounts officer. We move to the all-day café in the lounge, and Raman Rao orders coffee with idly and vada sambar for himself and coffee for me. Bhruha settles for water. I notice that Bhruha is a pretty woman. She is short and a little overweight. But she compensates for this shortcoming with a pleasant face and a million-watt smile. She is wearing a printed cotton saree and is having a tough time adjusting her pallu, which is blown by the draft from an air-conditioning vent nearby. However much she tried to cover her ample bosom, I could not resist noticing some soft flesh at the end of her neck whenever the breeze obliged me.

I explained the committee's decisions to them and requested him to lie low for sixty days and then reject the LOI on the grounds of validity.

A pleasant voice in the form of Bhruha speaks, 'Are you sure that the EMD shall not be confiscated?'

'I have the details given by my Chief Finance Officer on which I am banking. You need not worry on that ground.'

Raman Rao doesn't participate in the discussions, busy enjoying his breakfast and watching his mobile simultaneously.

'How about the new tender? What assurance can you give us on that?' asks Bhruha.

'I can only have a verbal commitment on the matter. As you know, this is confidential and cannot be given any written assurance. You have to believe me.'

'I think, Bhruha, you better meet the CE to get reassurance on what this gentleman is promising us.' Raman Rao finally speaks. He later apologises for receiving a sudden text message for a long pending meeting with an industrialist and leaves.

Bhruha and I spend a little more time. We indulge in small talk about the difficulties the government officials have in trying to manage the conflicting needs of politicians and the administrative rules and yet deliver. I tell her I shall intimate her as soon as I fix an appointment with the CE. We exchange telephone numbers and part.

After a few days, late in the evening, I accompanied Bhruha to meet Parthasarathy, our Chief Engineer, when he was about to leave office. Bhruha had to wait an hour to meet him even though I had fixed a prior appointment. She was annoyed, did not hide her displeasure, and lamented the government officials' lack of courtesy, especially towards vendors and contractors.

'Thank you, sir, for meeting me despite your busy schedule,' says Bhruha, hiding her irritation.

'It's ok. I hear from Venkat that your firm wants assurance about the Gauribidnur tender.'

'Yes, it was guaranteed by Venkat Sir while negotiating with us on the withdrawal of the present contract.'

'You see, madam, ours is a government organisation that follows the laws, acts and rules set by the administration. When a tender is called for, we have no control over who bids and who would be the winning bidder. However, we have tricks to tweak some clauses to favour a genuine need without circumventing the rules. In that context, Venkat had promised to ensure that in the Gauribidnur substation, we shall take care of your interest to compensate your loss.'

'But sir, what if we wouldn't be the lowest?'

'Madam, all the bidders in our corporation are known to us as they have been helping us design, construct and maintain the city's infrastructure. We have mutual respect as we need each other. It is a symbiotic relationship. If you don't qualify for the tender, we can persuade the winning bidder to off-load that part of the contract to you commensurate with what you have quoted in this Thimmalahalli tender. The Gauribidnur tender is twice the size of this contract, and there will be ample scope to employ your services.'

With that not-so-transparent assurance, Bhruha and I came out of the CE's chambers.

'What sort of assurance is this? How can we act on this purely verbal commitment? Can it be depended upon?' she lamented out of the earshot of the conference room members.

'Beyond what CE said, no one else can reconfirm. You have to have trust. Simple.'

I am now beginning to doubt her intentions. I want to spend more time with her to understand her thought process. It had become imperative, as it all depended on how Bhruha briefs her boss.

As she did not have transport to go back, I volunteered to drop her home, which is not on the way to my home, but I wanted to oblige her to understand her thought process on the future course of the action her boss might take. My driver has still not resumed duty, and I had to drive. She apologises for being rude and thanks me for agreeing to drop her home. All along the drive, I found her to be frank as she talked about her job and told me how she came to work for Raman Rao.

Bhruha Kandala is a childless widow. Her husband died in a factory accident near Mumbai, where he was working in a petrochemical unit. He was a chemical engineer, and some unexpected explosion triggered a chain reaction. A portion of the factory burnt to ashes along with twenty workers, two supervisors and Mr Kandala. Not able to manage the cost of living in Mumbai, she shifted back to her hometown, Bengaluru. She has her flat in Cox Town and, being a commerce graduate found employment with Raman Rao, with whom she was associated for close to five years. She learnt all the nuances of government tenders with the help of her boss and now appears well versed in handling contracts, though not technically qualified.

We now approached her home, and she thanked me and got down. I was about to restart the engine when she came to my side of the SUV and said, ‘Why don’t you come inside and have coffee?’

I agreed and parked the Toyota in the visitor’s parking lot as directed by her and followed her to her flat. I noticed that she must be around the same age as Lalitha – in her late forties – a strikingly handsome woman with a lithesome walk, notwithstanding the extra muscle on her body. Her hair is lightly marked with grey strands.

‘Please sit and make yourself comfortable. I will be back in a minute,’ Bhruha says.

A few minutes later, she returns as I engross myself in the décor of the front room, which is functional without being too opulent. She redid her makeup, rearranged her hair into a bun, changed into salwar kameez, and sat next to me. She wore a perfume which was strong and yet pleasant.

‘My flat is small. Only one bedroom and hall. I don’t have any visitors or even family members who visit me. So this small flat is ok for me.’

I am trying to understand why she is explaining to me. I nod and mumble something equivalent to *it doesn’t matter as long as you are comfortable.*

She gets up. ‘I’m going to make some coffee for you. It is late in the evening, but coffee should be ok? Right?’

I nod. I follow Bhruha to her compact and orderly kitchen while she puts the kettle on.

‘Sorry, I don’t have the decoction. Can I make tea instead?’

‘No issue. Anything is fine.’

I stand there in the kitchen and watch as she deftly pours hot water from the kettle, milk and tea powder into one container and lets it simmer and brew. She empties the contents into two earthen mugs through a tea strainer and mixes sugar – one teaspoon? Or two? I say two. I carry the mugs into the hall as she picks up the cookie jar and follows me.

I compliment her on her tea-making skills as I sip.

As we dunk the cookies in the tea and swallow, she shares her life in Mumbai.

'Do you know we were married for five years before that tragedy? I loved him a lot. We decided to have a child that year as he had an excellent offer from Aramco in Saudi Arabia, and we were about to relocate there.'

She begins to cry. I am not familiar with such a scene. I moved nearer to her and put my hand over her shoulder to soothe her.

She looked at me and said, 'I never opened up like this to anyone. I only have a boss-assistant relationship with Raman Rao and never discussed my problems with him. I don't know what came over me that I poured all my grief. I am sorry.'

As I hold her, I feel her cry. Nostalgic and tragic memories have come in a torrent as she explained her life in Mumbai. Holding her, I felt her getting closer to me, and I sensed her chest's softness on my elbow.

'It is getting dark; I have to go,' I say, trying to get out of her hold. Part of me is telling me, *'leave now!'* My external need overcomes the inner voice. I stay put.

She moved away, and her hand pushed my thigh to take a grip to get up. Instantly I discover my body is aroused. I involuntarily hug her and brush my hand over her hair to help her relax. She shifts closer in my arms and holds me tight to prevent me from moving away. I am increasingly becoming aware that she wants me here and now. Silently, I try to divert my mind but to no avail. She didn't leave my embrace, and I could hear a sigh.

Her move was tempting and exhilarating for a man who only shared a bed with a woman for a maximum of ten days in his entire life and never thought of sex outside his married life. I never for a moment felt it was not the right thing.

I turn her head by holding her hair, look at her face, and kiss her. She responds with a passion I had not experienced for nearly twenty years. I don't want to admit it, but I am having fun. She turns her whole body toward me. She slides a little closer. I stare at her for a moment. Isn't it odd? My head starts spinning.

I felt the same sexual excitement surge in her as I suggest we move into her bedroom. She agrees and pulls me in that direction. Before I knew it, we were in a solid embrace, and I tried to pull up her kameez, which was a bit tight. She volunteers, removes it with one jerk, and unclips her slip, exposing a mass of flesh. I can now see her soft, slightly saggy breasts. I have my hands on her breast, and she bent over me, letting me take her nipple and play with it with my tongue. *She is in a trance and forgets everything else around her.*

As I shed my clothes and exposed my hairy body, Bhruha ran her palm on my chest to feel the roughness of a man's hair. I can't resist anymore. I slipped my hand inside her open dress and covered her breast, enclosing it, locking her in. I lick her from her neck to her navel and caress her soft body to my heart's content. Her moaning adds to my pleasure. Before we knew it, we were both fully naked in her bed.

I let her move at her own pace until I hear her cry out, and then with my hands on her hips, I move into her until she makes a gasping sound that means I satisfy her.

Minutes later, passion extinguished, and we fell sideways, totally spent. It was almost 9 p.m. I bid goodbye to Bhruha, got out of her flat, and walked briskly towards my Toyota.

I am still in a daze as I climb into the vehicle and manoeuvre it through the traffic chaos to my home. As I relive the experience, my exhilaration has not waned. I remembered her words as I moved into her. 'Faster, Venkat, faster.' As my thrust continued with force, I noticed her breasts shaking up and down. I stopped for a second to lick the large areola around her nipple. She said, 'Venkat, don't stop. You can lick them later to your heart's content. Stroke hard now, man. Stroke hard.' I pushed deep into her and came with a thud. I almost fell on her in a heap and controlled myself as I slid by her side.

When I came back from the washroom, I found her spread-eagled naked on the bed with a smile on her face. She did not bother to cover herself. I could see her pubic hair wet with fluid droplets gleaming under the incandescent light. 'Thanks, Venkat,' she said as she slowly got up and hugged me tightly naked. Even though I was fully clothed, I felt her bare breasts' softness again arouse me. I quickly released her and moved away towards the apartment exit door. I waved as I left her home and blew a kiss on the way out.

A dormant urge has erupted. It has sprung forth like a geyser and refuses to be subdued. Initially, I felt angry with myself for changing the track of our marriage for something as trivial as sex. At the beginning of our marriage, I was prepared to content myself with vanilla sex if she was open to it. However, she rejected all my advances. But now, Bhruha opened a new vista in my life, and I found myself at the crossroads of a possible adulterous relationship. I wondered what happens when you offer yourself to someone and they open up to you.

By the time I reached home, it was almost ten thirty, and Lalitha was asleep. I could hear the TV sound in Kaveri's room. I tiptoed into the kitchen, ate what was in the covered vessels without bothering to microwave, climbed into my bed, and slept like a log.

* * *

Consequent to her rapport with Venkat, Bhruha convinced Raman Rao to accept the proposal of the Board. Thus, SVDC agreed to lie low and not push for the contract agreement initialisation for sixty days. At the end of the validity period of the tender, everything went as planned by Ambrish and Venkat. At CE's request, they called for a kick-off meeting with Bhogam Constructions to proceed with the design and construction. The Chairman and the Managing Director had already convinced Bhogam to accept the tender at L1 prices, promising a future quid-pro-quo.

Parthasarathy introduced Niranjan Agnihotri as the Director of Bhogam, who would handle the day-to-day work schedules and be one primary contact for all the issues concerning the site.

'Mr. Agnihotri, irrespective of what you have conceded on price, two matters are protected under any circumstances: completion time and delivery quality as per the tender's specs. Especially the latter. Our Venkatraman will be in-charge from our side, and in case of differences of opinion between you two, you may escalate the matter to me. I do hope it will not come to that.'

'You shall have no reason to complain on the aspect of the functionality of the substation. We shall not compromise on the quality of equipment used, and our construction methods shall ensure the safety of the equipment and deliver as per tender conditions – control and protection as in Substation language,' reassured Agnihotri.

Then the meeting continued to discuss the reworked milestone goals that are required to be fulfilled to ensure that the final closure of the contract shall be as per the original timeline.

'As you know, Mr Niranjan, we have lost over six weeks of precious time in executing the contract, reasons of which you are aware. To that extent, you must speed up your work,' added Venkatraman.

Chapter 8

I could convince my mom that my interest lay in job-oriented experience rather than pure academics. After my graduation in Electronics, I got campus placement as a member of the IT help desk team of a Baltimore-based Legal outsourcing company for their Bengaluru operations. Bengaluru handles the company's business east of Suez. I was trained in their head office in Baltimore and their most modern complex in Cupertino before they posted me to Bengaluru.

My company is a legal and financial consultant for Mergers and Acquisitions for their clients spread across the globe. In an acquisition, one company buys another company outright. A merger occurs when companies join together to create a new legal entity. Such M & A requires due diligence of the seller/collaborator. Sometimes the company does predatory diligence too. The company is proud of its security systems to ensure no data breach occurs, which is essential in its work.

We have redundant personal security, including biometric access into and out of any document review room. The data we produce and review stays in the company, and we are granted access to it remotely against strict protocols and time-tested SOPs. No cell phones are allowed in our document review rooms, and the computers are only connected to a local area network. The analysts do not have unrestricted access to the internet from the document review room. The computers are not hooked to a printer, and the USB ports are disabled. It is a dark environment. However, some access to select sites with prior approval by bosses and clearance by our team is allowed for the team's research work.

Recently one of our clients, desirous of acquiring another company for backward integration with our help, complained that they noticed the share price of their interested company had shot up beyond their original valuation, based on which they had outsourced the due diligence to our company. The customer complained that some data breach had occurred, resulting in a report in a Singapore-based financial tabloid alluding to the attempted poach. They claimed that this report could be responsible for the share upsurge. The client hinted that the data breach had occurred at our Bengaluru office. 'A situation report prepared by your team leaked through your so-called "Fort Knox" and found its way to a Singapore-based financial tabloid.' Baltimore immediately took cognizance of this and called for a video conference.

Being a senior team member, I was part of the meeting. At first, my boss, Aravind Goel, did not like the idea [of my attendance], as he felt I could be made the scapegoat and get fired. But our MD insisted.

Baltimore demanded, 'How could this happen?'

Before Bengaluru could respond, Cupertino butted in, 'Richard, if I may. Presently let us concentrate on beefing up our systems; autopsy can wait. Dousing the fire is the immediate need and not how the fire originated, though also we should investigate ASAP.'

'I think we are jumping the gun. For all we know, the leak may have occurred from the Bengaluru office. Someone may have tipped off the reporter of the Tabloid.'

That was Lin Yui, an American Chinese and the COO of their Cupertino office. Lin was the recruiter-in-chief during my campus selection. He grilled me close to three hours before he recommended me to Baltimore.

Bengaluru responded, 'Lin! That is an unfair suggestion. The position paper is a 32-page encrypted document. No way it can leave the office with the security systems we have adopted from Baltimore. We believe a malicious code has entered our system. If you read the tabloid report carefully, you will notice that the reporter cleverly used only particular significant paras from the doc – verbatim – intertwined with his interpretation and came to a conclusion.'

Baltimore said, 'Aravind, I understand. And I fully agree with you. Mark, I note your point too. Rakesh, I think our network security audit and improving the sterile atmosphere is the foremost need. I will be sending Williams to help you with the task. Whom are you recommending to support from your side? Also, Richard will send Martha to help you on the investigation side. I need this inquiry report of how this happened in one week. Martha can leave tomorrow as she has a five-year multiple-entry visa to India.'

Bengaluru said, 'Kaveri will be assisting Williams in finding ways to improve our present systems. If necessary, we may look in the market for better network security than we have. Comparison of Profiles – the Current Profile and Target Profile – may reveal gaps to be addressed to meet risk-mitigating objectives. An action plan to address these gaps to fulfil our company objective shall be presented within fifteen days. Aravind will lead the investigation team with Martha. If our Security protocols are inadequate, we have to find one with a deep packet inspection feature. But this new feature will inspect all data packets entering and leaving our networks to check for malicious code, malware and other network security threats.

Cupertino added, 'Our team recently came across a Bengaluru-based start-up with well-documented Frameworks for an impregnable Firewall system. I will ask Gogoi to brief Williams on that. I forget this firm's name, but a story appeared in the Infosecurity blog and CSO online regarding this Firewall. Rakesh, please study this before you finalise changing the present systems.

Bengaluru agreed, 'Sure. I will personally look into it.'

The meeting closed with a promise by the team for a daily report on the improvement plan and the progress of the inquiry.

That was how Salus Cyber Security Solutions headed by one Mr Athreya, had come to our organisation. We thoroughly studied the company's product and interacted with other users listed on their portal before we called him for a one-to-one meeting. I also gathered some interesting information on the founder.

Athreya is a finish coder. He is an artist with binary codes. He can be vocal and quiet at the same time. Give him a platform to talk about Cyber Security; he will surpass a seasoned politician in convincing you that the product and service his company – Salus Cyber Security Solutions – provide is the best in business. In all his introductions, he gives the origin of his company name. In ancient Rome, the goddess Salus was the personification of security, prosperity and well-being of both the individual and the state, publicly and privately.

He is an addict when it comes to his craft. He will burn the midnight oil for nights together if he smells that some geek on the dark web is prowling to attack. For Athreya, it is the work, not the client, that is critical.

As a founder member of Salus Cyber Security Solutions, his firm had many mergers or outright sale offers. He and his partner Ganesan had decided it was still not the right opportunity to sell. As they earned profits, they convinced their original investor and venture capitalist Kothari to divest some of his stake, which they bought. Ganesan, Athreya and another friend of theirs, Gaurinath, hold over 60% of the total equity as a consortium.

The product Athreya's team is marketed under the brand name BrookShield. His company's promotional site enlightens how it visualises traffic in real-time with drill downs to individual sessions by identifying abnormal and malicious in-flows and out-flows.

Athreya believes that a firewall's job isn't just to inspect incoming traffic; it should also ensure nothing unexpected leaves the network. In their experience, many enterprise firewalls are configured to scan traffic coming in but neglect to monitor the data leaving the network. This is a dream scenario for a cyber-criminal!

Athreya, the most vociferous member of Salus, is the most sought-after speaker in any workshops dealing with Network Security. MacAfee, Norton and such popular cyber security firms seek his advice on the latest threats and the patches that need to be updated. Without compromising on his own establishment's business, he volunteers when it is in the public interest – especially if it involves threats to State Portals.

Athreya was led to the conference room by my tech team before I entered. As he strides across my desk, I notice that he walks in measured steps, always contemplating God knows what. Athreya is wearing dark grey pants with a white shirt duly tucked in. He is tall by Indian standards and has a goatee. It sits nicely on him. His shirt pocket bulges with the latest iPhone.

This man can move pretty women to tears by ignoring them. The kind of guy you want to be on your side if you are in an altercation. I soon learned that he possessed that special gift for explaining rudimentary operational matters in simple language to the users.

We discussed how their product could help map risk to actual threats and better comply with security mandates such as the US's cybersecurity executive order. He confirmed that his software conforms to National Institute of Standards and Technology (NIST) framework models and standards such as NISTIR 8183 – NISTIR 8374 etc.

Williams is impressed by Athreya and his team member Ganesan and their background. Especially Athreya's work with Microsoft on Windows defender. Later Cupertino sent in their assessment of Salus from their contacts in the US. They were all positive, and we decided to further test their system. Williams and my boss Aravind's only worry is their team strength.

'They are still working from a café, and we are not sure of the efficacy of their product, though all the online reports have been very encouraging,' said Aravind.

On Cupertino's suggestion, we proceeded further with Salus.

At the conclusion meeting, I was absent as I had taken a week off to attend to my ailing attaih-paati.

My boss, Aravind, had called Athreya and his team to close negotiations and schedule the workflow. After pleasantries, they started negotiation for the service he came to sell us. We had many interactions on the tech aspect, so this meeting was on customisation, price, training and the after-sales services regarding updates and future patches. So, my presence was not needed.

I missed the final handshake. I need not have regretted it. Athreya ensured.

Chapter 9

Much to my parent's surprise, I was transferred from Seattle to Bengaluru. My mom has already started pushing for my marriage. I had to tell her to wait as I had other plans on my career graph.

By nature being restless and knowing that the new millennium needs a new approach to one's career, I decided it was time for a course correction in my career graph.

I was looking for an opportunity to go solo.

I say, 'Listen, Sten, I need to tell you something. It is something I should have told you a while ago.' Srinivasan Ganesan gained the title 'Sten,' as he talks like a nonstop firing machine gun.

After his postgrad from Michigan, Ganesan joined Microsoft, their development centre in Bengaluru. That was how we became colleagues at Microsoft.

We worked as a team for over three years in the company's Craft Supplier Intelligence Ecosystem, developing risk-mitigating software modules. Our contribution to Windows Defender software is well acknowledged in the company.

He is staring at his screen. I am staring into an unfinished coffee.

'These people make silly errors; it is exasperating to check every subroutine.'

'Sten, this is important. Something you need to know. I decided to quit.'

He turns. He looks me dead in the eye. He taps his head hard as though I have taken a decision that impacted him. And then suddenly, screams and made everyone in the hall look up. Then he quietly says, 'Athreya, you have the world, man! You are going solo, great. This calls for a celebration.'

Now I have the full attention of Sten.

I explained in short then and in detail later about Kothari and my plans with him.

Kothari was my hostel mate at IIT, Mumbai, where I was doing my PG in computer science. He was a wizard with hardware. He had a small Mumbai company manufacturing high-tech PCBs for prestigious clients like DRDL and ISRO. Apart from that, to sustain the development work, which was a long process of trial and error, he had custom-made billing and storage packages for the small and tiny sectors under the brand name K-Count. The brand had become famous for its ease of use by unskilled counter girls at the service counters of malls and other grocery stores. This sector's income helped him concentrate on his more significant project without worrying about his daily bread.

I talked to Sten about my plans to join Kothari and develop my Product, which I had been working on quietly for some time. I later introduced Sten to Gaurinath Pandey.

Gauri always dresses as though he has an appointment with a CEO of a large conglomerate. His father, an IAS officer, Bihar cadre, worked across the country. He could afford to send his son to the US to specialise in information technology-related courses. He excelled there with high A's. He published papers that other writers often cite. I met him at an IT conference in San Diego, and we have become friends. Persuaded by his mother, Gaurinath shifted back to India and joined Wipro. By coincidence, Wipro and Microsoft have some collaborative works which revived our relationship.

I convinced Gaurinath to be a room partner in the flat, where I shared the room with one other gentleman. Dipankar Banerjee, a chartered accountant, who insisted that two members' contribution for the upkeep of the apartment would not be enough to sustain the maintenance expenses as we wanted to have a full-time cook and maid along with high-end communication systems to enable us to work at home too. So, I requested that Gaurinath be the third member of our flat in Sanjayanagara, to which he readily agreed.

I tried to persuade Gauri also to join me in my new endeavour. But Gauri said the situation was not ripe enough for him to quit Wipro but will help in testing in his spare time. Being a roommate was a blessing as we could work long nights.

That was how we formed Salus Cyber Security Solutions, with Kothari as the investor. It did not take long to convince Sten to join us full-time.

Data breaches are a headache to companies that work in a competitive environment. Even famous companies like Yahoo, LinkedIn and Alibaba had data breaches that implicated millions of clients. Social media breaches are one thing, but corporate intelligence leaks are quite another. Athreya's team developed a Firewall as a marketable product, becoming the industry norm for all internet-dependent companies. Firewalls are a combination of software and hardware that work as a filtration system for the data attempting to enter your computer or network—firewalls scan packets for malicious code or attack vectors that have already been identified as established threats. Should a data packet be flagged and determined to be a security risk, the firewall prevents it from entering the network or reaching your computer. Their system was such that Kothari's team working in Mumbai could not penetrate it. The Product was widely accepted by financial institutes, Defence contractors and other IT-related businesses. Kothari was happy with this association and had given the team a free hand and stock in his parent company. Athreya was the guest speaker at every software-related conference. He constantly tweaked the system for future security threats and was always one step ahead of the fraudsters. Whichever firm bought the Product, Athreya's team would install the system and train the staff on the software's usage and other nuances. He often went to client sites to demonstrate, market or service the product. His continuous value additions to the product made the company earn enormous profits. Gaurinath could not yet firm up his courage and join their company full-time. Ganesan and Athreya did not pressurise him, as they understood his dad's attitude toward a salaried job. But he was a team member, nevertheless.

We were visiting a Baltimore-based legal advisory outsourcing company's Bengaluru office at their request. They had some data breaches reported, which almost cost them a client. We were asked to present our Firewall system, which they learnt from their Cupertino office with whom we interacted a few months ago. Our Firewall software has already become a best-seller. It has a five-star rating in a couple of international magazines and assessment portals, such as App Developer, CSO online, S D times, and Journal of systems and software, just to name a few.

Ganesan and I were waiting with our laptops for the meeting to start in their conference room.

He glances up reflexively from his laptop screen and finds a familiar figure passing the room. It took no time to realise who it was. How can he forget that small twenty-minute ride with her, with whom he had an instant connect? That day she wore blue pants with a white top with a slight flowery image on the right. Her hair was done in a bun, and she was nervously looking out of the taxi window and turning her head like a spectator in a tennis match. He noticed her have an angular chin with a tiny red dot between her eyebrows, which did not match her western dress. He shared a UBER ride with her. When not watching through the car window, she was busy reading emails on her mobile and did not acknowledge his presence. Or so he thought.

Today she is in a salwar suit. Her makeup was minimal, and he thought she needed none. He cranes his neck and waits for her to return to her seat, past the conference room where he was asked to wait for whoever is marked to see him and discuss the project. He waves to her from the glass partition as soon as she notices him. She smiles back, acknowledging his salutation.

He later learnt that she was the head of the IT helpdesk of the company. The other team members stroll with her into the conference room for the meeting.

The conference room door is winged open. She walked in with her team and sat at the far end of the table, letting her team sit facing us. She wants to maintain a low profile.

That was how I got introduced to Kaveri. She oversaw the Network helpdesk of the company. I had never seen a woman so gorgeous. I am a seller here; I wish I am a suitor. I felt like touching her, though we are ten feet apart.

She looks at me on cue.

I smile. She reciprocates very pleasantly. If she were playing tennis, she would be Steffi Graf. Fluid, graceful and technically excellent.

She was seated far end from us in the conference room.

We start our pitch. 'Salus Cyber Security Solutions helps organisations choose and use secure software and hardware.

If your current security system is hindering your service to customers, delaying reporting, or running on dated technology, we can help you through the evaluation and selection process.

I want to impress her with my Product. She is delicate; smart, and almost everything she says or asks is interesting. Tall in stature, cosy in attire, warm in manner. Nobody can blame me if I fall in love with her.

I notice that she is a senior team member; her boss is prompting her to ask us more queries. She took the floor as smoothly as Steffi Graf did with her forehand. A slice and I net. Fortunately, Ganesan answers as I fumble.

At lunchtime, Ganesan and I talked about Kaveri as though we had come to select a bride and not sell Firewall software.

* * *

We are given another shot at the demo in her office the next day. We bring our trial pack to run on their systems. It had enough checks to prevent them from copying or duplicating. Now we find ourselves alone with Kaveri. Ganesan wisely takes his phone and leaves the room to answer a mock call. We are now one-to-one. The Product provides a distraction for my interaction. She is too focused. I try for small talk.

'How long have you been working here?'

'Over two years.' Staccato reply and goes back to professional talk.

During coffee and lunch breaks, we chatted about our matters: family, academic efforts, hobbies and the like—just a polite inquiry, not too personal.

After an hour, she calls her boss and a few other team members into the conference room.

She briefed the members about what we achieved in the meeting. We said goodbye after an hour of tech talk and promised to be in touch for further buying, installation, and training progress.

Her boss values Kaveri's assessment of our Product.

After a couple of days, I call her. She picks up on the second ring.

'Hi, it's Athreya. I just wanted to ask whether your staff are comfortable using our evaluation kit.'

That's an excuse. I just wanted to hear her voice.

'I have not checked. I will get back tomorrow.' She cuts the phone.

I see Ganesan sniggering. I throw a pencil at him in mock anger.

After a few more meetings with their staff, in which I could not find Kaveri, they placed the order for multi-user product assembly for all their units. I am desperate to meet her. I wonder whether she has been taken off the negation team or changed jobs. I have no way of knowing without exposing my silly agenda.

But somehow, Ganesan sensing my predicament, found out that Kaveri had not left the organisation but had an emergency at home and was on leave.

Once we receive the contract, the process of customising the software, training their personnel, and redesigning the MIS to suit the culture of the organisation starts; this is handled by Ganesan usually. As I could not hide my longing for Kaveri, he asked me to take up the job, hoping that mere association with Kaveri might calm my mind.

'So that you can be more helpful to Salus Cyber Security Solutions than you were the past two weeks,' he says, hinting at my restlessness of not seeing Kaveri.

After a few meetings, though our discussions were centred on technical matters, I came to like her. If I had a tail, it would wag. If you are a photographer, you must simply say, 'Kaveri,' to make me smile.

* * *

I give her a birthday card and say, 'Happy Birthday.'

She takes the card, looks at it and asks, 'how do you know it is my birthday? Am I wearing something very gaudy?'

'No, nothing of the sort. I just know.' *Nothing is private for a smart IT guy nowadays. There is enough data free in the world-wide-net.*

'Thank you,' she says and walks around the table to sit at the usual table at the far end.

The next day, I took a step further. 'Can I call you for dinner this weekend?'

'What is special about this?'

'I want to thank you for recommending us to your firm.'

'I am not the only decision maker. We are a team.'

'Yes, of course. But you are the prime mover.'

'Okay, if you want to invite me for dinner. But not this weekend. I am going to Mysore with my friends.' *I was wondering when I will have a personal interaction with her.*

One more week passes. I don't see her in the training sessions. I'm in agony. I can't sleep. I can't think.

That Saturday morning, when it was still daybreak, I got a call from her.

'Hello?'

'Hi, Kaveri.'

'I am ready to cash the rain check.'

'Today?' while talking to her, I keep walking around the perimeter of our hall. Gaurinath asks me to stop. He is sure I will kick a chair's leg and hurt myself.

'Yeah. Are you busy?'

'No, not at all. I will call you and fix a time and venue.'

I enter my room and lock myself in to evade Gaurinath's sniggering.

'Fine.'

'I don't want any misunderstanding. I need to say this; you are beautiful. I admire you and would love to get to know you better. That is my only agenda.'

'You can tell me all that when we meet.'

I am on cloud nine – as the cliché goes. I struck a chord.

'I don't want to be impolite and say something or take liberties. Just want to get to know you.'

'Okay, with me.' And she cuts the phone.

After that day, we often met on weekends and weekdays after work.

When he initially invited me for dinner, I felt odd. But I liked the guy. What the heck? I want to enjoy the lingering experience of a proper date. Why not make friends?

I shut my eyes, put my head in my hands, and thought if he touched me, put his arm around me, held my hand, and put his mouth on my mouth, I wouldn't hate it. When he took hold of my hand to guide my laptop's mouse to the image he wanted me to see, I hadn't minded. My friends would know what to do in this situation, but I didn't. What sort of thoughts are these?

That was how it started. We hit it off—lots of common interests. Stage plays. Live music in concert halls. Cheering sports participants in stadiums. Reading Bios. Detesting TV news anchors. Watching Hollywood thrillers in theatres. And one common regret too. Cross-country trekking. But we also reconciled to it, taking refuge in our academic pressures, family attitudes and later work timelines. But we vowed that we should take time off someday with our respective partners to attend to this wish. The only thing that did not gel with me was his penchant for watching re-runs of tennis and cricket matches on YouTube.

And then we met often on weekends, as we started enjoying each other's company. We had gone to a movie I can't remember, and he held my hand the whole time and sucked my fingers sensuously. I thought I would melt in my seat and wanted him so much.

Athreya talked about himself, his family and Salus. He spoke of being a child playing with toy trains, his obsession, being a teenager and overcoming the reluctance to follow his father's profession.

Whenever he went home, which was once in three months or so, his mom rushed towards the door, sprinting with her arms spread wide. She greeted him as though he was recently released from lengthy incarceration for a crime he did not commit. Dad trailed her, playing it cool, as dads do. He inquired about his work and all. 'Can I cook your fav potato fry? Or stuffed Brinjal[7]?' asks

7. Egg plant/Aubergine

his dad. His mom never cooked. She was a career woman. They had hired help most of the time; sometimes, dad cooked. *Dad is an amazing cook. He keeps innovating new dishes – especially Italian. Whenever we went to dinner at Little Italy in Jubilee Hills, dad sneaks inside the kitchen, learns a new recipe, and experiments at home. More often than not, it comes out excellent with his signature touch.*

Kaveri listened. She was funny and interactive, asking more questions about him and taking him in as though what he said mattered. He saw more in her; he saw something honest; she cared. He talked, and she spoke, and he learned about her and she about him.

Kaveri shared her parent's uneasy marital relationship with Athreya and wondered how the concept of marriage would survive the newfound live-in concept.

My mother is beautiful; I inherited her looks. Though not entirely. But there is something about her, maybe older, with a sort of a finished look. She is elegant and proud, and I am not.

My parents lived like strangers, as though they barely knew each other. But my father always had time for me, while my mother, lovely and restless, was mysteriously busy and seldom had time for me. My appa, as I call him, would sit and talk to me by the hour, telling me about his job and how electricity passes from the power station to homes. And it did not occur to me until years later that he talked to me because he had no one else with whom to share things with. After school, after finishing homework, I would wait for my appa to come back and watch him work with drawings and make some lines, curves (he called them clouds) and comments with a pencil.

On my cousin's suggestion, I sent my parents to Kodai for their 25th anniversary. They ended up coming back early. I asked amma later. She had told me they'd run out of things to talk about after about one day. There were many activities in the Resort, but they did not care to participate. And they did not have anything they liked to do together. The Resort organised simple walking trips into the woods. They did not participate in any such activity too. They'd just grown apart.

* * *

Upon her wish, on a Saturday, I took her to my apartment in Sanjayanagara. She wanted to observe my living style. As soon as I opened the door, I heard a gasp. Gaurinath was half nude, wearing only shorts. After seeing Kaveri, he rushed to his room to change. When he returned, I could feel his annoyance for not informing him in advance of our visit.

'This is Gaurinath Pandey, our tester. He works for Wipro and helps us part-time,' I say.

'Hi.'

'Hi.' And went back to his laptop, punching furiously.

I gave her a quick tour of the house. I explained our work culture.

'We have another roommate, Dipankar Banerjee, presently on vacation.'

'Does he also work for your company?'

'No, he is a chartered accountant and just our roommate.'

'Where does Ganesan live?'

'He lives in RT Nagar with his parents.'

We compared the rooms of the bachelor and that of the family. She was surprised about the upkeep of our pad.

'We have a maid who does all the work, including cooking. She is good. She has a key to the apartment, so she comes and goes at her convenience.'

'Oh, isn't that risky? I mean, leaving the place to a maid?'

'Normally, your apprehensions are valid. But in this case, Dipankar has arranged a job for her husband in his office, and we pool up to ensure her three sons are educated by paying their school fees. That is how we bought her loyalty.'

Gaurinath butted, addressing me, 'Can we offer her some tea?'

She smiled at him and said, 'Coffee if it's okay.'

I wanted to be a good host and make coffee for her, and we drank it in the kitchen. We exchanged small talk on housemaids, and l listened to her office gossip.

She saw a stack of magazines on the front room table, picked up the Journal of systems and software, flipped it, and found a write-up on our Firewall systems. She congratulated us.

Meanwhile, her phone vibrated. She talked and cut the phone.

'I have to rush, that is my appa. It seems my attaih paati has suddenly become breathless, and they took her to hospital.'

She left soon by Uber.

I heard Gauri giggle.

'Come, man; you have gone too far,' he says.

I ignore him and go back to my room, pondering our frequent interactions for the past few weeks.

During our official interactions, I learned that she is intelligent, diligent, and a stickler for detail. Yet, she kept up her girly nature intact. Especially when she smiles; she has fascinating questions just to tease me.

'Why have matchboxes not become obsolete?'

‘Why do badminton players often blow at the end of their racket like a windpipe?’

‘Do you know why Amazon has a curved arrow below their brand name? The arrow starts with “a” and ends at “z” to say that they have everything from A to Z in their stores.’

‘Why do the elevators not have toggle buttons? So that, in case we press a wrong floor, we can erase by toggling again.’

‘What is this craze in cricket statistics if ground sizes are not uniform? A four can be three in a bigger ground.’

And so on ...

I added one to her questions.

‘If the men’s section of the restroom dispenses condoms, does the women’s section dispense morning-after pills?’

‘You are incorrigible with one track mind,’ she said.

We heard that her attaih paati died, and we offer our condolences. She said she missed her.

‘When both my parents were busy with their respective professions, she was the one who took care of me. When I returned from school in the evening, she fed and groomed me and helped with my homework. You know she was a retired school teacher.’

* * *

Our contract with Kaveri’s company is coming to an end. The last invoice was raised and paid. I got busy too. Our business is inundated with inquiries. We had our usual team meeting at CCD[8] to discuss the forward path of our company, which is now taking off. We decided we needed a bigger and more formal office space,

8. Café Coffee Day – a popular meeting place with free Wi-Fi.

and many alternatives were discussed. At that time, Kothari was relocating to Manyata Tech Park and offered to give us his old office. We were just about to disperse when Ganesan teased me, 'Will you be missing Kaveri now that our contract is made?'

'Don't worry; he has made enough arrangements not to miss her. They are now formally dating. You know, he invited her to our bachelor pad the other day,' Gauri blurted out.

'Chupa Rustom[9]! You didn't tell me about this?' said Ganesan in mock anger.

We met one Sunday to see a play at Rang Shankara. He wore a plain blue shirt and jeans. He seemed more handsome than I had seen him before. He smelled of a light aftershave cologne, which I can't identify.

He said,' I think we should meet our parents.'

'Is this your way of proposing to me?' I began to allow myself to plan for my future with Athreya.

He smiled shyly. We were already familiar with each other's families. His dad is a chartered accountant in a large pharmaceutical company, and his mom is a professor of economics at a college. His father is on the verge of retirement.

He casually informed, 'Once we have furnished and staffed our new office and are settled, I want to buy a proper house and bring my parents to Bengaluru.'

We decided that I should meet his parents first before I introduced him to my parents.

---

9. C*hupa Rustam'* is a common Hindi phrase attributed to a person used to convey the hidden complexity of a personality which is usually shy.

His parents are expected to come to Bengaluru in the third week to attend a wedding, and we decided it should be the right moment to introduce me to them. He said he never discussed me with his parents, although he is close to his mom.

'Neither did I. Dating is not acceptable in our society. I am defying customs by meeting you regularly,' I say.

After the show, we returned to our respective homes in separate cabs as it was late in the night to have dinner.

When he fell asleep, he dreamed about Kaveri.

Chapter 10

When Karthik returned from Scotland, he could not show any proof of educational achievements, which annoyed his dad. However, he managed a letter from the College Admin that he attended the course. Once his sickness ruse got exposed, Sheshadri confronted his son.

'I don't know what you did all these years. And for all that expense, you have this to show?' he growled, dangling the certificate of attendance.

After that, Sheshadri did not speak to his son for ten days. Through his mother, Karthik convinced his dad he was interested in being self-employed and pursuing some business. His mother persuaded Sheshadri to part with five million as seed capital to start a real estate consultancy. His Chikkappa, already in real estate, helped fix up contacts for him to start. Karthik began as a home loan consultant, a symbiotic arrangement with his Chikkappa as he also wanted help for his clients to buy the property he was constructing. With the help of his dad's office legal assistants, he quickly learnt the ropes of getting bank loans for Chikkappa's clients.

Within one year, Karthik partnered with a small firm run by his friend – brokering apartments. Soon the business expanded, and Karthik owned an office. Marriage was the last thing on his mind. He found that it was unnecessary botheration. Instead, he befriended many girls on the pretext of marriage and gained sexual favour. But Lalitha continued to haunt him. He could not locate her in the lane where she lived, as neighbours said they shifted to God knows where.

Karthik's longing for Lalitha had become an obsession. She besotted him. He searched for her, contacting all his erstwhile classmates of both genders. But of no avail. Days passed into years.

I am now forty-two years old. I lived my life remaining as a spinster. I carry morning-after-pills when I go to parties, not the rubber sheath that spoils the pleasure. That way, I avoid embarrassing surprises. I currently live alone. Always a loner. My mother has long left me to her peaceful destination, away from my dad's scrutiny. My dad lives in his world of crime and punishment. I hardly interact with him except when my Chikkappa wants some advice on a settlement with BBMP.

If you compare it with other real estate businesses, I have the best office space in town. Once in a way, like all of you, I also think it would be nice if someone brought me a coffee with a smile and not as a chore. Someone to talk about my day. It never happened for reasons that are difficult to convey. The simplest version is that I could not find the right person. My mother tried too. But my reputation within our family preceded me. The more intricate version would require a long narration of opportunities that I blew up. Add a failed marriage. My wife said I abused her sexually, insisting on unnatural sex. Finally, she left me with my child. My friend tells me that I am afraid of lengthy and meaningful relationships. Of course, he has not seen the inside of me, which longs for Lalitha.

By now, she must be in her forties. She must have turned more graceful with age. She may have married with children too. So, what if she is married and has an adult child?

One of my new year's resolutions had been to try to stop the search for her, as finding her in this big city is almost impossible. There were just too many places to look, and the chances of ever seeing Lalitha were very dim. But even as I reminded myself of that resolution, a persistent voice whispered inside my head that one of the reasons I had been on the lookout was my hope of finding her.

And then it happened.

I am going up the escalator in Mantri mall when I notice her coming down. The resemblance is striking. The same swan neck, with long hair, she possessed all the qualities of a fairy walking down. And like Lalitha, I notice she has the same gait when I turn around to see her walk toward the turnstile exit. Instinctively I decide to follow her. I jump up the escalator two steps at a time, turn around and repeat the same feat coming down. I could catch her at the entrance trying to persuade autos to take her to her destination. I noted three auto-rickshaws refused to accept her fare. I find a fourth passenger-less auto coming from my right, and I wave to the driver to stop. When he stops, I tell him, shoving a hundred rupees note in his hand, 'Do you see the lady in green salwar and white dupatta? Please take her to whatever destination she wants without asking questions.' I also pushed a slip with my telephone number and asked him to send me the address where he would drop her off. He looks at me with a question mark. 'I am an inspector in mufti. I am required to follow her,' I say with mock confidence. Without further questions, he quickly starts his engine and moves towards my Lalitha's doppelganger.

It takes over two hours to receive the call from the driver. Eventually, when he did, I was relieved to know the address was that of a residential locality. Convinced that I was a genuine inspector, the auto man also sent the location on my WhatsApp.

I reach the place guided by my Sat-Nav. The address doesn't give the house number but only the coordinates. I crane all around me continuously. I am hoping that from some house nearby she will appear. I waited in my car; for how long, I lost count. I walk around the street like a stray dog—an apartment complex opposite me and an independent house, and then another apartment house. From the apartment complex left of the bungalow, I watch a young couple walk out, each carrying a bag. A moment later, an elderly couple exited. Her bag slips from her shoulder, and he pushes it back up for her. A mother and a hopping teenager are the next to leave, and then a grandfather and two small girls.

Yet, no trace of her.

After three days of the vigil, I hear the creek sound of a gate of an independent bungalow. I see a woman in maid attire pushing the entrance gate open and a lady entering the driver's seat of a Santro. I couldn't see her face as she bent while climbing onto her seat. But I am in luck. The car door re-opens, and the lady comes out of the car and re-enters the house to fetch something she ought to carry in her car. Even then, I can only see her buttocks, yet I note the tall structure of a typical south Indian lady. I quickly repositioned myself to take a better view of when she would reappear from the door of her home. An attractive woman in her early forties shows up, and I can see her unmissable in her entire regale personality. Lalitha aged gracefully. While she was about to climb into the driver's seat, she looked up and across, and our eyes met—my Casablanca[10] *moment. We look at each other for a few seconds. Now I can see that she is trying to place me, looking towards me and away. I am glad that my face is still, in a way, recognisable. I hope it holds the blueprint of my longing for her. She identifies me as much as I did her, so I presume. My Lalitha might have grown in years, but she is still my passion. However, I can never pardon her for making a mockery of my life. I was almost incarcerated. It had been nearly twenty-five years since I last saw her on that fateful day when I tried to confront her, trying to convince her to marry me.*

10. *"Of all the gin joints, in all the towns, in all the world, she walks into mine."*

I drive every day to her home and park my SUV and wait for her to appear. To have a glance at her. I found her timing odd. She is home till 3 p.m., then she moves to where I don't know. Following her in the chaotic traffic of Bengaluru is a waste of time. I lost her within a few minutes of driving behind her. Now that I know her timings, I park my red Honda at around 3 p.m. and watch her climb into her car and go away. The more I see her, the more I long. She appeared to be a settled housewife. But she made a mess of my life. I can't forgive her for what she has reduced me to. For the last few days, I have seen her door locked. Maybe she went out on vacation. I gave up on her and promised myself that this obsession should now stop.

Lalitha often noticed the red SUV parked opposite her house. A recent occurrence. She didn't know the make of the car. The car is parked there only in the afternoons. Morning times it was not to be seen. Also, when she returned from dance class, it was not there either. She ignored it as a coincidence presuming that it might belong to the opposite home of a businessman. She knew the businessman's wife and wanted to inquire about it but thought otherwise, as it would embarrass her; it could be interpreted as an intrusion into their privacy.

But today, when she was about to climb into her Santro to go to her Dance School, she observed a vaguely familiar figure lurking near the red SUV looking at her. It disturbed her. *Where did I see this gentleman?* She wanted to bring the same to the notice of Venkat but forgot all about it in her busy schedule.

Chapter 11

Kaveri leaves her house an hour later than initially scheduled.

She opens the Uber app, types a Sanjayanagara address and waits for the taxi to arrive. There is a slight drizzle. She hopes the rain won't surge; otherwise, one can get stuck together on the Bengaluru roads for hours.

'Wait,' her appa says from the doorstep. 'Wait, I can drop you.' That is the last thing she wants.

'It's okay, appa; the Uber driver has already accepted my booking.'

Her voice drowns in the sudden heavy downpour. And Venkat watches his daughter in jeans and a top to match, walking briskly towards the waiting taxi.

'How should I dress?' she asked Athreya when it was decided that he would introduce Kaveri to his parents when they were expected to visit him at his Daffodils apartment, Sanjayanagara.

'How do I know such things? You are beautiful in anything you wear. Just wear what makes you comfortable. My folks are modern enough.'

* * *

It is raining harder now. Kaveri runs down the pathway and into the lift corridor of the apartment complex. She tries to shake off the dampness. Kaveri pushes three on the lift panel and looks at herself in the lift mirror. Part of her dress and hair is wet – even though it is a small distance from the taxi to the apartment. *I better go straight to the toilet and rearrange myself to be presentable.*

Athreya opens the door and moves away to let her in.

'I want to go to the washroom,' she says without waiting for him to react.

'Let me get you something to dry off with,' he says and hands her a towel.

She stares at her face in the washbasin mirror. She tries to superimpose the face of Athreya next to her and notes that they made a good couple.

When she came two weeks back to the apartment, she found the place quite neat – very unlike a bachelor pad. Athreya already told her he had two more residents with whom he was sharing the accommodation. Gaurinath Pandey from Bihar and Dipankar Banerjee from Bengal. Three rooms with attached shower and toilets, a kitchen and a big hall. It could be expensive, she thought. All of them being in IT/software industry domains, these expenses are a pittance. The front hall had no furniture save a dining table and a sofa whose tapestry appeared worn out. At the far end of the room, she found a large table, two swivel chairs with two desk-top computers and other infra with wires all over and the WIFI flickering intermittently. WFH set up.

She comes back into the front room and announces, 'Sorry. I am late. My appa's cousin, Chittappa,[11] had come to visit us. They are from the US. They came to see their daughter, who is in Bengaluru and married to a doctor. My Chittappa – first cousin of my appa – was very close to my appa since very young. So he

11. Father's brother in Tamil

took this opportunity to pay respects to his brother. My parents forced me to wait until they arrived. They had not seen me since I was a kid. So I had to stay put. You were texting me to rush. I couldn't even answer you. Sorry. But it was beyond me.'

'Also, this sudden storm added to the traffic woes. I was pushing the driver, but he also could not do much. Incidentally, I don't see your parents. They haven't arrived yet?' asked Kaveri.

'They had come immediately after their lunch feast of the wedding, at about 3 p.m. My parents had a flight at 7 p.m. to catch. So, they had to leave earlier than scheduled because we feared that this unexpected storm might delay their ride to the airport,' he said apologetically.

'I am so sorry; I missed them. All my fault. I was eagerly waiting to be introduced to your parents today.'

'Not to worry. Such things happen. We can go to Hyderabad and see them there,' Athreya suggested.

'That appears to be the only solution.'

'As I told you earlier, I don't want to pronounce our decision on the phone without them meeting you one-to-one.' Athreya feels depressed suddenly.

'I understand.'

'Let me make some hot tea for you.' Athreya goes inside the kitchen while Kaveri relaxes in the hall. She hears a vessel clanking on the floor and rushes to see what caused it. Athreya looked down at the spilt milk and said, 'there goes your tea.'

They have a hearty laugh.

He pins her to the wall as they move toward the living room. Holding her breath, she presses her spine more firmly to the wall, waiting for him to make the first move. She wonders how a woman like her, who never allowed any man into her life, could be so vulnerable as to invite a kiss from a man who was a stranger until four months ago. He moves quickly and kisses her. She opens her mouth, letting him in. Her mouth is quite soft. Suddenly she loses all her rigidness, and her body inclines towards him. He does what feels natural to him; hugs her. She let her arms crawl around his neck, dragging him closer. Her rain-soaked hair sticks to him like a sponge. He laughs and moves to brush it away. She pushes him away smilingly.

'Your roommates may arrive. Let us be careful.'

'Dipankar has gone on a motorcycle expedition to Sikkim. Gaurinath has gone to Gurgaon for a client meeting. He will return after four days.'

'Did you plan all this to seduce me?' she said smilingly with a twinkle in her eye.

Without answering her, he hugs her and she hugs him back, gripping him fiercely.

Athreya pulls her to the sofa. Before she becomes aware of what is happening to her, his hands are exploring the inners of her top; she helps by loosening her tight bra. He gets up and leads her to his room and bed. She follows him like a zombie, dazed. He slowly undresses her, teasing her of her navel size, and she is so wet down there. She is embarrassed, and he puts her down on his bed and kisses her all over with little licking kisses. She comes to rest atop him; her wet hair tickles his nostrils, and he sneezes. She laughs out loud and falls on her back beside him invitingly.

Be good, she says. *I don't want to do this. You do, you do.* She grabs his head and brings it to her neck. *Here.* He licks, and she moans. He strokes her face lightly. She looks at him with half-closed bleary eyes. *Come.*

Seeing the full length of his muscular body, he resembles a film actor she knew; she kisses him lightly, lovingly. His body seems to surround her; she feels she is disappearing into him. He kisses her cheek, her closed eyelashes, and then her mouth, his tongue moving over hers, making it his. A low moan escapes her, her tongue meets his, and they both know they need each other.

And then, without a word, he is inside her, pounding into her. *Slow, slow, I am not going anywhere.* And suddenly, he is still and falls beside her, with his palm resting on her left breast.

They spend over an hour in the bed entwined. She is pleasantly surprised at the emotional intensity of his lovemaking.

Athreya takes hold of Kaveri's hands and pulls her up from the bed without speaking. He kisses her and retakes her into his arms, embracing her warmly. She clings to him and slants her head on his bare chest; her cheeks feel the sweat-filled hair. She feels her body trembling. After a few seconds, she draws away gently and looks at him. He feels an intense gaze with heavy, slightly moist eyelids. He at once knows that she is happy and yet confused.

'Come, dear, our conjugation is the result of our love,' he says with calm assurance.

'Yes, of course.' *She is a woman of few words.*

She is not overtly disturbed about the unexpected developments in their short relationship, which surprises him. He thinks she is the most natural person he has met. She is devoid of conceit, Honest to a fault.

'Let me go. It is already late, and my appa has been messaging me,' she said calmly, as though what happened between them was a natural result of their bond.

Athreya gets up; goes into the washroom to get dressed. As he comes out, he notices she is all set, ready to go, while adjusting her violet-coloured top to straighten the crease.

He watches Kaveri intensely as she adjusts her hair: graceful, elegant and self-assured, and he realises that his life would be worthless without her.

A bird cawed. The rain continues to splash on the window glass. The sound resembles a soft song that he liked.

She doesn't appear to feel any remorse or guilt. I shouldn't, either. I love her more than ever.

Kaveri rejects his suggestion to wait for the rain to stop. She wants to move out immediately and reach home before her parents worry about her and call her up. Her appa especially. She takes out her mobile and pushes the Uber app. She waits after typing her address, but the app simply goes in circles to match the drivers with riders.

After some time, a message: 'No Uber drivers are available now. Try after some time.'

She panics and looks at Athreya for a solution. Meanwhile, miraculously the rain reduces to a minor drizzle.

'Now that the rain has almost stopped, I can drop you off by bike.'

'You have a bike?'

'It is not mine. It's Dipankar's. He is a bike freak. He has a state-of-the-art one for biking expeditions and one for local travel. He took the heavy metal one to Sikkim; the other is in the parking lot. I can give you a ride back on that. But I don't have a raincoat.'

'It's okay. Waiting any longer for the rain to fully subside will only consume time; it is getting dark, and I don't want my appa worried and call all and sundry in my friend circle.'

'As you wish, my dear.' It made her feel like Athreya was somehow in control of her happiness.

Suddenly, there is a power outage. The auto-UPS battery power of their apartment comes on. But the building power is not connected to any backup, so it was dark in the corridor, and the lift was not functioning. Athreya ran down the stairs to the basement to pick up Banerjee's mobike and asks Kaveri to come down after locking the front door, *the key behind the door on a hinge*. She locks the door and hops down the stairs.

She checks her watch. Umpteenth time. Dinner time. Amma and Appa are expecting her. She eagerly waits for Athreya to come out of the basement. As the bike engine roars towards her, she notices that he is wearing a helmet unstrapped. She quickly mounts on the pillion seat, with legs on one side and holds him tight. He looks at her and gives a thumbs-up, locks the straps of the hood and engages the gear. The rain has miraculously abated to a minor drizzle.

They are still a little high when he drives her toward her home. Though the rain subsided, the street lights were off, and it is pitch dark on the streets. When the bike drifts across the empty road, it terrifies her, and she tells him to slow down. He stops and looks at her and says, 'sorry.' Then he drives moderately slow, not in silence, but in an animated discussion about their future, and when he jokes about their impending nights, she laughs. She notices a car behind, focusing with bright blinding headlights, and she hugs him tighter.

Chapter 12

The sand heap on the pavement spread across the road and the adjoining lane because of the rain. The car from the left lane skidded on the sand and swerved right and left. Then the driver saw a motorbike coming with full headlights from the main street perpendicularly, blurring his vision. He pulled back to first gear and simultaneously pushed and released the clutch to make the vehicle stop instantly, which it did. The driver watched the bike slide and hit the right fender of his car, and the bike rider and the pillion were thrown off their vehicle. The car driver stopped and looked around. There was no one in the vicinity, and the street lights were off, too, because of a power outage. He saw the motorbike's driver fall on his chest, and he appeared motionless. His medical training came to his rescue, and he checked his pulse. Then he instinctively opened his mobile and checked google – *hospital near me* – and dialled the number given. The driver then dialled 100 and waited as a good citizen for the Ambulance to arrive. He then noticed a security guard walking away from the accident across the street and yelled at him, but the guard briskly went away without turning.

The constable, with a walkie-talkie, responded to an emergency call and rushed to the accident spot as directed by the caller. He parked his bike and bent over the man lying face down on the road. He appeared unconscious. No movement. He noticed another victim with her head on the pavement and the balance of the body on the road. A lady in her early twenties, the constable, noted. Her wristwatch stopped at 8:22. The constable, Veeranna, as the name tag showed, called for more help on his radio walkie-talkie and requested another colleague to the spot with a camera. Veeranna's colleague arrived riding pillion on a mobike driven by a man in civils, who climbed out quickly and started clicking photographs all around.

Veeranna then asked his colleague to note the driver's name and other details while they waited for the ambulance. The car driver informed Veeranna that he had already called for the ambulance.

The second constable noted the car driver's details in his diary:

Vivek Agnihotri, s/o Niranjan Agnihotri 352, 17th Main, 6th block, Koramanagala. Car no KA 84 MZ 2345, Blue Maruti Swift. He was surprised to note that his driving license was issued in the State of North Carolina, USA.

The ambulance staff eased the man's limp form onto a stretcher, into the back of the vehicle, and drove off with a blaring siren. The man in mufti stayed at the site with his mobike and camera. The ambulance had only one stretcher; the constable had to call another to take the other victim, lying at the other end of the street.

Vivek did what they taught him at the medical school. He did not venture to move the body other than noting the pulse. It is for the ambulance team to do their assigned roles. Vivek stayed put until the medics completed all the formalities; the wounded were taken into the vans, and he drove behind the ambulances as directed by the Constables.

They all arrived at the Emergency ramp of Ramaiah Memorial Hospital in less than ten mins. They quickly wheeled the two bodies from the rear entrance direct to the casualty ward.

The ward sister called for more help on the public address. The orderlies put both bodies on the benches of the rooms and freed the trolleys. The constables were asked to wait for further formalities.

The duty doctor was summoned from his canteen break. He had the nurse strip the injured man to the waist and the rest of the clothing – shoes, socks, belt, trousers, underwear etc. He could see a deep gash on the chest. And made a lengthier examination and found the body lifeless. Then he turned to attend to the other victim.

The two constables were on the phone with their inspector. The inspector directed them to look for evidence and to tag the man's items for identification. He was surprised to note that there was no wallet or mobile on the victim's person. The inspector called his colleague, and he was asked to rush to the accident site and recheck for any information that could lead to the victim's identity. Later, he briefed his SHO, kicked his motorcycle to life, and whizzed past the traffic to reach Ramaiah Memorial Hospital.

The inspector could not crack open the iPhone of the lady victim. With the help of her id card, he called the registered emergency contact number and informed the person on the other side of the phone to rush to the hospital without giving too much information.

We found this number from the lady's ID card who is involved in an accident and is in Ramaiah Memorial Hospital. Please come over soon.

The inspector noted the victim's name as Kaveri Venkatraman and informed the registry office of the Emergency cell.

The inspector wondered whether the car driver was responsible for the accident as, evidently, the bike driver might have panicked, noticing the erratically shaking car from the left lane onto his path.

While the emergency staff were doing their assigned duties, the Inspector called Vivek to ask a few questions. He introduced himself as Manjunatha, attached to Sahakaranagara Police Station. He instructed his constable to check Vivek's alcohol level by breathalyser, and no traces were found.

Manjunatha inquired whether Vivek was acquainted with the bike riders.

'No,' he said

'They are strangers to you?'

He nodded.

'Then what made you get involved, knowing fully well that the Police may suspect you of being the reason for the accident?'

'I did what I felt right at that moment. Nothing else mattered to me then.'

'What you did by calling the Police and Ambulance was a nice gesture,' the Inspector said. 'You can go now, but we shall keep the car for forensic study. You can pick it up later if our team finds nothing incriminating. From what I heard from you and the beat constable, you may be innocent,' added the Inspector.

Vivek had no alternative but to agree to leave the car behind. He hailed an Uber and went home.

* * *

As soon as a relative of the lady victim, identified as the victim's father, Venkatraman, arrived, the emergency room staff first led him to the duty doctor. The hospital recorded the victim's name as Kaveri from the information provided by the constables.

Dr Biswajeet Panda introduced himself and noted the visitor's name and his relationship with the victim. Dr Panda insisted that Mr Manjunatha be present during this meeting.

'Our Ambulance brought your daughter to the hospital at about 9:55 p.m., as per the records. We have checked her vitals, and she is responding well to the treatment.'

Dr Panda explained the procedures they have carried out in the emergency room as per the standard protocols of the hospital. He reassured the couple that she was well taken care of, and as there was no external injury, except some scratches on her elbow and the right knee, she could be home soon. Dr Panda added that the patient was not responding to the stimulus was a worry, and a senior Neurosurgeon was investigating.

Manjunatha then took over and explained the accident as they reconstructed from the eyewitness and the situation the police found at the site.

* * *

Venkatraman, now joined by his wife, Lalitha, asked Dr Panda whether he could see their daughter. The doctor called the Head Nurse and instructed her to lead them to the ward to see their daughter and to fully brief them.

The attending Emergency team updated them about the steps the staff took in the aftermath of the accident to reassure them that the hospital had taken every precaution necessary to resuscitate the patient.

'First aid for an unconscious trauma victim at the scene of the accident is directed toward securing the vital functions (ABC = airway, breathing, circulation). We controlled the manifest bleeding. Suppose the neurological examination reveals that the patient is unconscious; in that case, a consensus of medical opinion holds that the patient should be intubated without delay, as clinical experience has shown that swallowing and breathing are often impaired in comatose patients. Their airways are in danger of inhalation of blood, secretions, or vomitus. The neurological examination is the basis for further interventions after arrival in the hospital. That is when we call the Neuro Surgeon,' the doctor said.

'Fortunately, this hospital has both CT (computerised tomography) and magnetic resonance imaging (MRI) because there may be an accompanying spinal cord injury. The unconscious patient's bodily posture and brainstem reflexes indicate whether the lesion lies in the brainstem or the cerebral hemispheres. We are yet to come to such a diagnosis. He added that the patient is being shifted to ICCU for further examination and monitoring.

The cubicle they positioned Kaveri in is self-contained, with a small sink. Screens are attached at all ends of the bed – left, right, and foot. She had tubes running from her neck to a container, another tube ostensibly a feed channel for medication and nutrition. There was a stool, but visitors were not allowed to sit for more than ten minutes without making any sound. The nurse station was not far from the bed where Kaveri was sleeping. From the crevice of the partially drawn curtain, the nurse would ensure that the visitor's activities are monitored as much as the patient's. Venkatraman's eyes flickered around the room to other beds. A couple in their fifties had an animated conversation with the head nurse. An older man and a woman – from her countenance, almost certainly his wife.

* * *

We have been simply waiting in the hospital corridor since the day of the accident. The doctors were not forthcoming in appraising us on further updates on my Ponni. My parent-in-laws had come to give us company and pray with us. We hardly slept a wink. When hungry, we went to the hospital canteen to grab a sandwich or a dosa to survive. We are too scared to go home, except for a change of clothes.

I find a kind soul in a white coat while having coffee in the canteen. He is the resident doctor, Dr Biswajeet Panda, attached to the ICCU, where Kaveri is presently sleeping peacefully. In the eyes of ordinary people like me, doctors are at the top of any pecking order. Hardly amenable to opening up, frankly. Dr Panda appears different. I could easily converse while he is having lunch and I holding my coffee mug. I start the conversation by introducing myself as the father of his patient, Kaveri. Reluctantly but lucidly, he speaks. He is a PG intern.

'Generally, most patients at a hospital come out of a coma,' he says reassuringly, 'typically, a coma does not last more than a few days or a couple of weeks. In some rare cases, a person might stay in a coma for several weeks, months or even years.

Depending on what caused the person to go into a coma, some patients can return to their everyday lives after leaving the hospital.'

'Thanks, that gives me some solace. Do these patients remember what happened during and before the coma after they are in their senses?'

'Sometimes, someone who comes out of a coma can remember what happened to them and resume their normal activities. In other cases, a coma patient might need therapy to re-learn basic tasks and functions, like tying their shoes, even some motor skills such as putting a morsel in their mouth etc. And learning to talk as before. It is possible for people who have been in a coma to make progress and improve their quality of life.'

I thank him and leave the cafeteria with a less burdened mind. There is some hope.

* * *

Today is already the third day of the accident.

The call from the Head Nurse from the ICCU brings both hope and trepidation. Hope: my Ponni is responding to stimulus and could be discharged soon. Trepidation: I fear the coma has turned into a brain-dead case. Lalitha, an incorrigible optimist, would not want me to think of anything negative. So, I refrain from discussing my thought process with her. In such situations, you need a friend – not an idiosyncratic life partner.

The Head Nurse informs us that Dr Ingalhalikar would like to talk to us.

We sit outside Dr Ingalhalikar, Neurosurgeon's room, in a regimented queue as the hospital staff calls. We were clueless about the status of my daughter. Fortunately, this call gave us some hope for positive information.

The doctor's assistant now directs us into the room while he handed us a file to carry inside. We had met the Surgeon earlier in the ICCU when he came for his regular checks. His manner, tone, and diction changed from patient to patient. He was gruff with some, gentle with others, amused, concerned or impatient according to his appraisal of what the patient needed.

The doctor gesticulates for us to sit while he is responding to a caller, who, from the doctor's response, appears to be annoying him. After listening to him patiently, he says okay, cuts off the mobile, and turns to us with an inviting smile. He quickly picks up the file, glances through it, and turns the pages. He uses magnifying glasses to read.

'So, you are Kaveri's parents. Have we met before?'

'Yes, briefly,' I say.

'Okay, let's come straight to the point. Firstly, I assure you that your daughter is in safe hands and responding to the feed and ventilator support, though she continues to be in a coma.'

'Could you explain further, sir,' says my wife in a soft, pleading voice.

'Our Duty staff and the nurses would have already briefed you on the course of action we have taken and intend to take to ensure the best possible care for your daughter.'

'Yes, sir, they did. But we would like to know what the current status is.'

'We all agree that the patient is in a coma. Let me explain the coma status, so you understand the patient's condition. The scientific explanation of coma is based on the Glasgow Coma Scale. It has three parameters to judge the condition of the patient. Eye Response, Motor Response and Verbal Response. On all these parameters, your daughter scored the lowest. However, in motor response yesterday, we found the score to improve to what we call "Extending". It means there was a slight elbow movement in an external pain stimulation. That is an improvement,' he said.

'The Glasgow Coma Score is insufficient documentation of the patient's neurological condition. In an unconscious patient, the pupillary responses must be examined, as well as the motor function of all four limbs (tested separately). The patient's (lack of) spontaneous movement, response to noxious stimuli, and any pathological flexion or extension responses are to be noted. These findings are crucially important, as they have a bearing on the differential diagnostic considerations in patients with brain and spinal cord injuries. An attending radiologist interpreted a CT scan of the neck, including sagittal and coronal reconstructions, as negative. In pure English, no severe damage has occurred to the patient. We are at a loss to know why your daughter is still in a coma.'

We find ourselves no wiser than we were before. Noticing our body language, Dr Ingalhalikar continued, 'we need her to be in observation for a few more days. Our duty doctors regularly contact me to inform me of the patient's progress.'

We are back to our chairs in the lounge. My mom-in-law brings us some food which we gulp. She tells us to pray to Ganesha and that everything will be fine.

I am completely disturbed about the position Kaveri is in, and it makes me contemplate. I reason that what seemed to be an accident is God's way of punishing me for my adulterous relationship with Bhruha. I am sinful. All the family is suffering because of my one indiscretion. It's God's anger. I don't know how to repent. Will my penance bring my Ponni back to normalcy? Dear God, I'd never been unfaithful to my wife in all the 23 years we'd been married. Though we've just fallen into dull domesticity too quickly, I love my wife. All those years, I hoped for a sign of sexual warmth, just one spontaneous sign that she recognised me as a man. I never gave up hope until that day when Bhruha invited me to her apartment. Then for the first time, I saw a woman who came close to me, behaving like a woman. Perhaps not as a woman should behave with a married man. But we both were in dire need of companionship. Please pardon me for just this one indiscretion. Leave my child alone. Please.

I doze off the chair as we wait for the night to turn to day.

Careful. Don't jump, walk.

She has now picked up a pebble-like thing from a heap of gravel lying on the pavement. While sieving the mixture of various rock fragments, the quarry owners run them in a trommel, which, apart from sieving, acts as a ball mill to reduce the size when required. Sometimes a sharp rock piece gets stuck in a corner and shaven repeatedly, making the sharp corners into smooth stone like a pebble from a beach. A rare occurrence. Ponni could locate one in the heap of irregular stones. She has a sharp eye.

Taking her to school is an education for me. Lugging her bag and snack box, I have to constantly answer her queries, tumbling out with every breath and also ensure that she is aware of the side road crossings. She always remembers what I said. The next day she added more about things I had not seen or noticed. Why is the man pushing his cycle instead of riding it? I say it is uphill, and he can't peddle. She thrives on adventure. Parenting her requires patience. Lots.

We go past a stationery shop. She insists on buying an India map. Her teacher told her to draw as many rivers as possible from their origin to the sea. Did my name come from a river? Yes, dear. Kaveri flows through two South Indian states – Karnataka and Tamil Nadu. And it's also called Ponni; that is how your nickname came from. My teacher tells me it flows from west to east.

We are running late. I push her to move quickly without looking around for exotic objects, which will slow us down. She reluctantly agrees, and we reach school.

Lalitha's kitchen work and dance classes come in the way of dropping and picking Ponni. Being a government employee has advantages – you can mix home and office comfortably. The maid drops her off when I am on tour, and my driver picks her up. Lalitha could take up the extra workload of her school, knowing Mangamma or Subbaih is there to do the school runs when I am not around.

My bond with Kaveri has grown much more than just a parent and child. As years went by, I almost became her confidant. My attaih, or Lalitha, sorts her gender-related issues as per convenience.

Lalitha and I had only Kaveri in common unless you counted Lalitha's run-ins with my attaih.

Another day, another school drop. I must do this for the next two months—no official tours. Every year July to August, Lalitha has her dance classes in the US. Money bag NRIs want their children to be updated in Indian culture. If you can teach Indian music and Indian dance and have a reputation built over the years, you can mint dollars. Lalitha makes more money in three months than I do in a year. Fortunately, this period is monsoon time in India. Not much site work. Also, labour goes to their villages for sowing. No inspection site visits for me. Advantage Lalitha.

'Up the slope, I run.' Kaveri drifts from my grasp. And she slips. I drop her bag and tiffin box and pick her up to examine the damage. Nothing. Just a tiny bruise on the palm. She doesn't cry. She looks at me, smiling. She never cries. Strong girl. I scoop up the bag and fill the contents spilt on the pavement. I am about to stuff the doll – rabbit – into the bag. She snatches it from me and hugs me to her bosom. That is comforting for her. I walk her to the school and hand her over to her class teacher, Miss Vandana, to ensure her bruise is taken care of.

By the time Lalitha returns from the USA, the wound will have healed. I don't have to give any explanation of my 'clumsiness'.

* * *

The mobile sound wakes Venkat up. He looks at the watch. It is early 6 a.m. He looks for his wife and finds that Lalitha is not around. She *may have gone to the washroom.* He glances at the incoming call, an unknown number with no name. He turns it off by swiping the red icon. *But which call centre calls early morning?* He walks up to the ICCU and finds the guard who has a look that says, *don't attempt to come in; I will not allow it.*

Chapter 13

Venkat's phone beeps once more. This time, he answers and says, 'Hello. Who is this?'

'I am Saakshi Gargi from the Bengaluru Chronicle. Am I speaking to Mr Venkatraman of Bengaluru Power Corporation?'

'Yes, what is it regarding?'

'What is your take on the incident at your substation, which has caused undue hardship to a poor farmer?'

'I'm not sure I understand what you're saying....' Before Venkat can finish his sentence, she cuts him off and says, 'So you're not regretful?'

'I'm sorry, I don't know who you are, and this is just gibberish to me.' Venkat switches off his phone.

Then he dials Gopala Krishna Murthy, his Executive Engineer. When the EE sees his boss's phone number on his mobile, he immediately picks up.

'Yes, sir. Good Morning. I hope Kaveri is recovering well.'

'Yeah, thanks. Has anything untoward happened at any of our substations?'

'How did you find out? We didn't want to bother you because you're on leave and dealing with a family crisis. A young man died in an unfortunate accident at our Thimmalahalli substation.'

'How could this have happened? Is this, by the way, the same job we gave the new contractor?' asked Venkat.

'Sir, yes.' He went over the entire incident in great detail.

A security guard discovered a shepherd's body near a transformer and alerted the engineer in charge of the substation. The substation was built on government land that local villagers used to graze cattle, sheep, and goats. A sheep shearing unit in the village outsources sheep rearing to local villagers in exchange for its business being set up on agricultural land.

A steel fence surrounds the substation to prevent people and animals from entering the premises. Lightning struck the fence during a stormy night. The fence's pole foundation sunk, and two consecutive poles tilted in opposite directions, creating a massive gap between the mesh and the foundation.

The following day, a sheep left its flock and entered the breached fence after mistaking green leaves painted on a wall of the substation room for vegetation. In search of the missing sheep, the shepherd entered the substation through the same fence opening to drive the sheep back to its herd.

While doing so, he walks on compromised earth. The engineer missed a weld shear on a copper strip attached to the transformer core test stud and grounding link. This weld failure caused EPR (Earth Potential Rise), in which an electric current entered the ground, creating electrical "pressure" that caused the soil to rise in voltage. The boy was killed because the conductive chain allowed voltage to be transferred from one zone (the substation) to another (the shepherd). This current disrupted the signals controlling the shepherd's heart, causing it to stop beating.

'What corrective steps have you taken?' asks Venkat.

'Sir, the villagers were agitated and refused to cremate the body till the government announced compensation. The corporation said it is the contractor's fault, and he has to compensate.'

'When did this happen?'

'It was last week, sir.'

'What is the latest on this?' asked Venkat.

'For the time being, to appease the local villagers, the government has agreed to compensation, which they claim will be deducted from the contractor's outstanding bills. These villagers are led by an opposition legislative member who wants to profit from the situation.'

'Ok. Thanks. I shall connect with you sometime this week when I get some free time from the hospital duties.'

* * *

The next day, Gopala Krishna calls on Venkat at the hospital. After prelim inquiries on his daughter's progress, he says, 'Did you see today's Bengaluru Chronicle?'

'No, I don't read that paper. Also, of late, I am not in the mood to read newspapers; I browse them when I find them in the waiting lounge, but without much interest.'

'I understand, sir. I did, however, purchase a copy for you to read. You must read this report because our Chairman is very upset about what was published. He asked me to check with you to see if you could come to the office for a day to discuss this matter at any mutually convenient time. He wants this meeting to take place this week.'

EE thrusts the paper folded to magnify the specific report he wants to show his boss.

POWER CORPORATION NEGLIGENCE COSTS YOUTH'S LIFE

saakshi.gargi@bengaluruchronicle.com

A farmer's son grazing his sheep was found dead due to Bengaluru Power Corporation's negligence. Last week, a 17-year-old boy was killed by an electric shock at the BPC substation in Thimmalahalli.

The substation was reportedly shabbily fenced, with low-quality fencing and poor concreting, resulting in fence breaking. The boy went inside the fence to look for his sheep, who strayed through the broken fence.

Madhusudan Borla, the local MLA, has represented the deceased's parents, claiming that the fence did not meet regulatory requirements. 'The fence wasn't that high enough, and it wasn't even a fence,' he told the newspaper. 'It's just some low-quality barbed wire encircling the substation. Furthermore, the concrete poles supporting the fence were not properly embedded in the ground, resulting in a huge gap. The government engineers' supervision is inadequate. According to a BEC spokesperson, the power station is "surrounded by a seven-foot strong security fence, erected by an approved vendor for the corporation."

The villagers in the area refused to cremate the body until adequate compensation was announced. Even though the BEC initially stated that it was the contractor's responsibility, it was forced to back down. The contractor was unavailable for additional questioning.

More investigation is being conducted to uncover the corporation's functioning, which has recently come under fire due to frequent outages.

'This is too damaging. What do the CE and MD say?'

The Chairman has barred them from talking to the newspapers. He is waiting for a meeting with the Power Secretary for advice. Before he meets him, the Chairman wants to discuss with us,' said Gopala Krishna.

Chapter 14

This hardly had been the joyous homecoming they'd hoped. Kaveri returned with an IV stuck to her arm and a feeding tube. Keeping her in ICCU any longer was unlikely to be of much help, the doctors opined.

The Medics said parents must bide their time with recommended medication and artificial feeds. She requires routine monitoring. Feed her. Medicate her. Clean her. Exercise her limbs. Turn her to keep bedsores away. Beyond that, we must wait for her to come out of the coma. You can as well take her home along to assisted care facility. We shall be on call whenever needed.

Tears rolled down Venkat's face as he saw the limp body of his Ponni carried inside his home. She is alive – that's all matters. He kept reminding himself that he should feel relieved. The doctors promised she would come out of the coma, but no specific dates were given.

Lalitha is calmer. But we both know this isn't over. Our girl will be her ebullient self soon. However, there could be side effects. In every case, there was at least some memory loss. But studies suggested that this was transient. But what if Kaveri does not conform to the statistics?

* * *

Lalitha notices that it is almost two months since Kaveri has been in a coma. After forty days in ICCU, she had been home the rest of the time. She wonders when Kaveri had her last period. She called the hospital head nurse to check whether they had noticed any vaginal discharge indicating menses. Negative. Lalitha panics and consults her family doctor, Smita Vartak. The doctor asks her to do the pregnancy test first, which jolts Lalitha but she does as told. It's negative. Lalitha is relieved and informs Dr Vartak.

'She is comatose, and amenorrhea (no menses) can be because of trauma. Let us wait for a few days more, and we shall do an ultrasound,' the doctor says.

Lalitha decides not to share this information with Venkatraman. She vaguely remembered that Venkat's Bengaluru Power Corporation office got entangled with a police case concerning a contractor executing works under Venkatraman's supervision. She does not want to burden him yet, on a still uncertain matter.

* * *

Venkat listens in total disbelief to Lalitha's abridged account of Kaveri's missing periods, the need to take her to the hospital for an ultrasound, and more.

The Ambulance staff wheels the patient into the examination room and asks Venkat to wait and let Lalitha be present. The hospital gynaecologist, Dr Vardhan, had been briefed by Dr Smita Vartak on the matter. Dr Vardhan found that transabdominal ultrasound did not give a clear picture. He decides on Transvaginal ultrasound. Dr Vardhan notes a growing foetus and makes the observations: Gestational age: 11 weeks approx. Foetal heart action present: 150bpm. The baby, or foetus, is now around 41mm long from head to bottom. The head is still supersized, but the body is growing quickly. The fingers and toes are separating. There are tiny fingernails and small ears.

'I must congratulate the presence of mind of the mother for quickly bringing the matter to our notice. I know nursing staff and doctors who have missed pregnancy in the emergency room multiple times. I remember one patient who came in with seizures. She was put in the ICU, and nobody thought her big belly might mean she was pregnant,' said Dr Vardhan, addressing no one in the examination room.

Hearing this news, Lalitha is shocked, and her mind goes blank. She comes out of the examination room and briefs Venkat. Venkat rushes inside the room where Dr Vardhan is still making the report and asks, 'are you sure about what we have just heard?'

'No doubt about that. The reproductive organs (the ovaries and the testes), which secret sex hormones, are outside the central nervous system, though the brain activates them. Pregnancy can occur even if the woman is in a coma. The baby is in good condition. We must inform the attending medical staff to re-examine the patient's feed as the foetus' nutritional needs also need to be considered.'

'She has a feeding tube. That helps with nutritional support, and babies tend to grow well even with just that. Unlike IV fluids, a feeding tube is surgically placed in the stomach instead of a vein and provides a formula for a patient,' Dr Vardhan adds.

He talks like a typical gynaecologist interested only in the health of the foetus and the mother, unconnected with what the parents are going through.

'We are shocked, sir. Can we talk to Dr Ingalhalikar and the other team members who attended her? We have too many questions,' pleads Venkat. Meanwhile, he hears Lalitha talking to her gynaecologist, Dr Smita Vartak, and he asks Lalitha to give the phone to Dr Vardhan to explain the matter to her. Dr Vardhan explains to the person on the other end in a detailed doctor-speak the observations he has made and gives the phone back to Lalitha.

'Lalitha, the findings of Dr Vardhan appear to be correct. Your daughter is pregnant. You have to accept this fact and take different decisions. If you need, I can come to the hospital after an hour to help you tackle the situation.' Lalitha thanks her and cuts the phone.

Noticing the confused look of the parents, Dr Vardhan suggests that they consult the Admin cum PRO of the Hospital for further directions.

Venkat rushes to the administrative manager of the Hospital, Prashant Reddy. Venkat knocks on the door and enters without waiting for permission. Reddy is a small man with thinning hair and a weak chin. He wears a white shirt tucked in white trousers and places himself on the swivel chair with crossed legs resting on a nearby stool, exposing his expensive sneakers. Venkatraman introduces himself and asks for a meeting with Dr Ingalhalikar, Dr Biswajeet Panda and Dr Vardhan. He peers at Venkat and says, 'Let me get the details before I can discuss this matter.'

Venkat briefs him. Reddy requires the official version before he makes any decision. He asks Venkat to wait in his room and rushes to ICCU to meet the staff there.

Reddy takes over an hour to return to his cabin. Lalitha accompanies Reddy and looks at Venkat, who is on the chair with his head in his palms. *You should have called me too!*

'We are all taken aback by the whole thing. My daughter was in your care from the day of the accident till she was shifted to our home, on the suggestion of your doctors,' said Lalitha.

'What are you suggesting?'

'We are confused. Our minds are not functioning,' said Venkat dulling the effect of the harsh tone of Lalitha.

'Are you hinting that she was raped during her stay in the Hospital? Let me rule out the possibility if you think this is another Aruna Shanbaug[12]. We have close-circuit cameras in the ICCU, where she was present from the morning of the day after the accident when she was shifted from the Emergency under the direction of the Neurosurgeon. You can check the same at any time. Our staff believe it could be a case of forced or consensual penetrative intercourse before the accident.'

The couple looks up with mouths agape.

Finally, they come to senses, and Lalitha asks, 'what should we do now?'

'Let me organise the meeting as your husband requested. It may take time. Please wait in the lounge so I can ping all three doctors and fix it. I understand the urgency, but we need time to arrange this.'

After close to three hours, the meeting is arranged. Apart from the doctors, the couple and the PRO, they find one another gentleman in the room. He is introduced as Mr Ranganathan, a medico-legal expert.

'We have re-examined the patient from a forensic angle to know whether she was assaulted before the accident. We found no marks, scratches or cuts on her body other than what we observed on the accident night. A bruise on her arm and knee appeared as the result of her body being dragged by the force of the throw from the mobike.' That is Dr Panda's briefing.

---

12. Aruna Shanbaug, while working as a junior nurse at King Edward Memorial Hospital, Mumbai, was sexually assaulted by a ward boy and remained in a vegetative state following the assault.

'So are you suggesting that the victim has consensual intercourse before the accident?' asks Dr

Ingalhalikar.

'Or she may have been drugged and raped,' opines Ranganathan.

'Yes, that is possible. But we have no way of knowing now. Almost eleven weeks have passed since she came to our hospital. Any forced substance abuse is now difficult to check, as we have been medicating her as a part of her treatment,' says Dr Panda.

'That is a matter of conjecture and requires police investigation. We can offer no other advice,' informs Reddy addressing the blank-faced couple.

'Therefore, we are only concerned with the health of the foetus growing inside the unconscious patient. As per our hospital's philosophy, we have to save every life at all costs,' said Dr Ingalhalikar.

No reaction from the couple. They are dumbstruck.

Then Dr Ingalhalikar explains the procedure from a neurological angle. He mostly repeats to the larger audience what he briefed the couple when they met him the morning after the accident. He adds some more:

There has been virtually no medical research on pregnancy's effect on a comatose woman. Understanding consciousness is one of the major unsolved problems in science. An ever more critical method of studying consciousness is to check disorders of consciousness, such as brain damage leading to coma, vegetative states, or minimally conscious states. First, the exploration of brain function in disorders of consciousness represents a unique lesion approach to the scientific study of consciousness. As soon as we know a given coma patient has a growing foetus, our ethical attitude towards it changes completely.

Whether or not vegetative or coma patients are conscious is an empirical issue that we do not yet know how to resolve. So deciding by anyone other than the patient their life-changing decisions – in this case, whether to abort a foetus or not – involves ethical and legal complications.

The couple had never experienced such gut-wrenching helplessness.

'Can we, as guardians of the patient, decide on the matter? Just hypothetically, as we have not decided to abort the foetus,' asks Lalitha in a mature and calm tone.

Ranganathan raises his hand to answer.

'There is no legal precedent or provision under any legislation for appointing a guardian for a person in a coma. Hence, you have no other alternative except to approach the Court under Article 226 of the Constitution of India, seeking extraordinary relief. The court must consider the interests of the mother and the unborn child; if it's found factually that an abortion is necessary to save a woman's life, then they would not object. The issue is whether an abortion is in her best interests.

Even if you go to court for a direction, the court will ask for a medical opinion on whether there is any danger to the child or the mother if the foetus grows. Depending on the mother and child's medical situation, we shall have to come to a conclusion at that time of court inquiry. However, hypothetically, if the court poses the question to us now, we shall say there is no danger to either the mother or the child. This is reconfirmed by Dr Vardhan also,' says Dr Ingalhalikar.

'Let me illustrate a typical case. A British woman spent three months in a coma and lost her memory after a horrific moped accident, but woke up to surprising news – she was 11 weeks pregnant. Doctors at the Hospital in Bristol broke the news of her pregnancy to her mother, and the family waited for her to wake up from her induced coma, which wiped all her memory from the prior three years, including the identity of the unborn child's father. Doctors said she would be unable to walk again – but after using a wheelchair for several months, the lady defied the odds and gave birth to her healthy baby boy. She also learned to walk again as her son took his first steps. Such miracles do happen. There are many more examples of such coma-induced patients living a normal life. Another famous case appeared in the NY times in 1989, strikingly similar to ours. The lady was pregnant when she went into a coma because of an accident. The case's issue was whether the husband should be appointed as the legal guardian and opt for an abortion if he so desires. I don't have complete case details, but one can dig them up. You only have to google,' added Dr Ingalhalikar.

'It is up to you to take a decision. Meanwhile, we suggest you keep your daughter in the hospital with us for close monitoring because of her coma status and the foetus's health. Despite many guidelines for returning to active life following mild head injury, it is difficult to give an affirmative answer without riders. However, you need not admit her into ICCU, but in a private room where you can have an arrangement for a live-in assistant if you wish. The private room is not as expensive as the ICCU bed. Dr Vardhan, our chief gynaecologist, has confirmed that the child is normal and growing well but requires proper nutritional care, which is only possible in a hospital environment,' opined Dr Panda.

The couple looked at each other. Lalitha asked, 'If we want to go to court to get permission for abortion, how much time do we have?

'Per the MTP act, the court can permit abortion up to 20 weeks and, in extraordinary circumstances, till 23 weeks. But as

Dr Ingalhalikar said, you require a medical opinion for abortion, even if you are appointed legal guardians. Also, the courts take such cases on a fast track. You may get a hearing sooner,' opined Ranganathan.

'My suggestion is that first, please examine the matter with the help of the police by recreating the entire accident. The police are well equipped today to do such complicated investigations. If it's consensual intercourse, your daughter may rebuke you for your presumptuous decisions after she wakes up from the coma,' warned Reddy.

Chapter 15

Kaveri's parents are now in the office of the Police Inspector, Manjunatha, as suggested by Prashant Reddy. They explain the purpose of their visit and request his help in finding out more about the accident from their diary reports on the matter. *Prashant Reddy had already briefed Manjunatha to cooperate fully with Kaveri's parents, giving him the background of their proposed visit.*

'We have handed over the body of the rider, one Mr Athreya, to his parents. It took over four days to find them.' He elucidates to them the difficulties he faced in finding the address of the dead person's parents.

Athreya's parents arrived from Hyderabad and went directly to the police station as directed. Manjunatha drove the grieving couple straight to Ramaiah Memorial Hospital. They were met by the PRO, who took them to the Morgue.

They were briefed on the accident while on the way.

'Why did you take four days to inform us of the accident?' asked the victim's mother.

'Madam, we could not find any identity on his person when the beat police reported the accident. Probably someone stole the wallet and his phone in the melee of the incident. We then tried to contact the owner of the mobike which your son was driving. The RTA registry showed the address of the mobike owner, but we found that

he was not living there as he had relocated to another apartment in Sanjayanagara. That took us time to trace him. When we did find his mobile number, we learned that the owner was on a trekking expedition in Sikkim. From the information we received from him, we went to his flat, where we met his roommate, Gaurinath Pandey. Pandey could find your address by hacking Athreya's laptop.'

'Gaurinath also contacted us on the phone yesterday,' the father informed. He also said my son could have been saved if police took him to a hospital quickly,' complained the father.

Gaurinath had told them more details of the accident on the phone as he had inquired from the neighbouring flat owners, who noticed the commotion on the street and were watching the process of shifting the bodies in an Ambulance. Gaurinath informed them that one lady was a pillion on the bike, had grievous injuries and was in a coma. Though Gaurinath could guess who the lady was, he decided not to give more details; neither did they ask. The grief of the loss of their son made them numb.

'We did our best within the infrastructure we have. Please note, sir, there was exceptionally heavy rain that day in Bengaluru,' pleaded Manjunatha.

The couple were inconsolable seeing the lifeless body of their son; hearts broken, shattered forever, and no amount of sympathy – no matter how sincere, could mend their loss. They were distraught. Neither of them could believe they would never be seeing him again.

The mother was inconsolable. Athreya was their only son. They had met him just a few days earlier - all bubbly and enthusiastic about his work and the accolades he was getting from his customers. When they broached the subject of his marriage, he said, 'Amma, when the time comes, I will inform.' They wished they had spent more time with him when they visited Bengaluru recently. The rain had forced them to rush to the Airport.

The Morgue Doctor said it would be appropriate if they could meet the pillion rider's family and console them. He informed them that the pillion lady was in a coma and was unlikely to survive. The Doctor recreated the possible reasons for the accident when handing over the body and the hospital's death certificate. He gave more details about the accident, which he learnt from the beat constable. The doctor said that the slippage of the motorcycle occurred not because of the vehicle's speed or the driver's negligence. The construction sand spread across the road from the pavement could be the cause.

The couple was reluctant to face the pillion rider's family as they felt their son was responsible for their distress. They could not muster the courage to apologise to the family.

After the formalities at the hospital, the couple decided to take the body to Hyderabad. With the help of the hospital staff, they arranged a refrigerated casket and an ambulance to proceed to Hyderabad. They accompanied the ambulance in another car as it would be uncomfortable to travel over 9 hrs in the ambulance.

* * *

Venkatraman and Lalitha want to meet the roommate of the rider on whose bike Kaveri was pillion riding when the accident occurred. On their request, Manjunatha dials Gaurinath Pandey. Gaurinath doesn't take up the call.

'Do you have his address?' Venkatraman asks.

'What purpose does it serve? I can find the parents' address, but they are in Hyderabad.'

'We want to know more about Athreya from his friend and his relationship with my daughter. Why was she pillion on his mobike? Friends know more about such matters than parents,' says Venkatraman.

'Sure, I can call him to come here. If you try to call him, he may not be forthcoming and evade meeting you, but he would surely come to a police station,' suggests Manjunatha.

'Incidentally, did you find any CC camera along the street?'

'It is a lane, not the main street, so no police or municipality-installed cameras. In the Sanjayanagara main street also we don't have cameras. The budget is sanctioned, but it is taking time to find a vendor. However, I can check whether there are any jewellery shops on the street. These shops usually have their own CCTV set up. I have not checked whether any private home nearby has any such security system,' says Manjunatha. Manjunatha calls his head constable to check for any CC-camera set up on the main street and report.

Then he dials the reception number noted from the Wipro portal on his mobile. The operator says Gaurinath is unavailable; *in a meeting*. He leaves a message to call back and gives her the number and name. He doesn't mention his designation as Inspector of Police; *receptionists are rumour-mongers.*

But he knows that Gaurinath would have the number saved under his name or designation and will surely call back. When they last met, Manjunatha indicated he might call him if more information was needed. The Inspector asks the couple to phone him again the next day so he can fix a meeting with the roommate of the bike rider.

In the evening, Gaurinath called Manjunatha.

'The parents of the lady who was pillion of your friend's bike want to meet you. When can you meet them?'

'I am free only on weekends. They can come to our apartment on Saturday morning,' says Gaurinath Pandey.

And he gives directions to their apartment. Daffodils, Off Rajgopal Road, 5th Main, Sanjayanagara.

'Our building is at the end of the cul-de-sac on the 5th Main. It's four-storeyed. We are on the third.'

* * *

On the appointed day, the couple drives to the 5th Main. Manjunatha could not accompany them as he had some other pressing engagements. But he insists that a person in uniform should accompany them whenever they meet Gaurinath.

Uniforms will make people talk, which they may not do as freely with civilians. As directed by the Inspector, Head Constable Veeranna is waiting near the apartment on his bike. They exchange greetings.

'Please call Gaurinath to come down. We don't want to go inside,' says Venkatraman.

Gaurinath appears on the balcony and waves the couple to come inside. But they are reluctant and signal him to come down.

'Do you know our daughter?' asks Lalitha.

'Yes, she had come once to our apartment on a Sunday. I spoke a few times to her on the telephone about work. That is all. Ganesan knows more about them.'

'Who is Ganesan?'

'Our partner. He lives in Malleshwaram. I can give you his number; you can talk to him.'

'How does Ganesan know her?'

'Our company, Salus Cyber Security Solutions, is a Vendor to your daughter's company. That is how we know her.'

'I thought you were working for Wipro?' asks Venkat incredulously.

'I am moonlighting with Salus.' Gaurinath suddenly looks down as if maybe he crossed the line and said something he shouldn't have.

'Were you aware that my daughter was visiting your apartment on that fateful day?'

'I was away at a client site in Gurgaon. I only knew that Athreya's parents would visit him that Sunday. Beyond that, I don't know anything,' Gaurinath adds with all sincerity. 'Sir, we lost an excellent partner and founder of our company. We are confused about how to go about further. I was about to join them full time too. And this unfortunate death has disturbed us. From what I heard from Athreya and Ganesan, your daughter was a smart and intelligent lady. We all miss her too. Please accept my condolence.' The couple notices a slight wetness in his eyes.

The couple thanks Gauri. Gaurinath walks up to his apartment complex and glances back before pressing the lift button.

After Gaurinath is out of their earshot, Veeranna says, 'If you think that something happened in the apartment on that day that shouldn't have, we can get a court warrant to search the place.'

'After so many months, what evidence can the police collect?' asked Lalitha.

'You will be surprised, madam.'

He explained an incident occurred in the precincts of Yelahanka PS.

A lady's body was found near the Yelahanka lake bed. The police found the body after a rag collector informed them. The lady wore a traditional dress – a saree and appeared to be from a well-to-do family. No other identity could be found. The body smelled awful. Rigour mortis had set in. There was no missing complaint of any lady in Yelahanka or any nearby PS. The lady's photo was splashed across the net and pasted on walls of the roads in and around Yelahanka. Fortunately, Yelahanka had a CC camera installed on a few main roads. A couple of malls in the area also had cameras facing the street for security purposes. And in one such search, the police found that the lady was coming from an independent bungalow. With the help of a court order, the police searched the house and questioned the inmates, who feigned ignorance. During the search, they found a toothed plastic comb with split hairs stuck in one of the cabinet drawers. They compared the DNA of the hair strands with that of the dead body and other household members. The DNA matched the deceased lady. Rest was a simple matter for the police to catch the culprit. But all this search took over four months, yet the hairs on the comb remained—sheer luck.

'Okay, let us come to that later; we want to visit the accident site. How far is it from this place?'

'About three kilometres,' says Veeranna.

'Incidentally, did you find any CC Cameras in the vicinity?' asks Venkat.

'None. This area is mostly residential locality.'

'Nevertheless, can we take a recce of the place by walking along the path the bike took that day? You may come by your motorcycle if you don't want to walk,' says Venkatraman.

Veeranna agreed to accompany them, and all three started walking from Daffodils to the accident site, observing every house.

In such matters, you need a lucky break. They had two.

A security camera on a pole is visible from the street. The house was a setback from the road, surrounded by a small fence and a carefully tended garden. The bell at the gate was at a height that required full stretch to ring.

An elderly gentleman opened a window, and seeing a constable in uniform, he opened the gate fully and let them in.

They introduced themselves and stated their purpose. The gentleman gave his name as Siddha Goud.

'The camera now is defunct. It needs repair. After about three months of staying with my son, I just returned from the US and noticed the malfunction. Sorry, I may not be of much help.'

'Sir, we need the images from around three months back; at that time, it might have been working,' says Venkat. A shot in the dark.

'Sir, on that day of the accident, there was a massive power outage for over two hours,' the perennially pessimistic Veeranna says.

'That is no problem. If the camera were working that day, it would function for over four hours without power as I have a backup battery setup.'

Police look for difficulties instead of finding solutions.

'Anyway, *let* me check,' Siddha Goud says and asks them to make themselves comfortable in the living room. A burly lady with snow-white hair and a frown on her face looks at them as though they are intruders who came to rob her.

'The camera has an SD card which records the information for about three months, as my son-in-law who installed this system told me. Hopefully, you may find some useful images. Let me get my laptop.'

For a man of his age, Siddha Goud appears computer-savvy. He inserts the card with the help of a card reader and opens the date-wise recording list. Luckily, the memory has the data of the day of the accident. Upon prompting by Venkat, the old gentleman opened the video from the evening of that fateful day.

The riders crossed the house at 8:16 p.m., as registered by the camera's timer. The entire span of 30 meters sweep of the camera took three secs from the bike appearance of the rider at the start of the sweep till out of range of the camera, i.e. 36KMPH, which could be considered normal.

They notice that the pillion is hugging the rider tight and animatedly talking and laughing. From the dress – a velvet-coloured top – Lalitha could guess it was their daughter, Kaveri. And also, her profile was clear. They wound and rewound and ran the film a few times more. They can't recognise the face, even by freezing the image. It's too grainy. But her wristwatch can be seen. Her countenance makes it clear that the lady was not unhappy or appeared distressed. Veeranna confirms that it was the same bike found at the accident site.

'I think we can now rest assured that the union was consensual,' said Venkatraman. Lalitha did not comment. She was lost in thought. Venkat mulled that one over. *It made sense, but it is still a shocking conclusion*. But he wasn't sure she had bought it entirely. 'I still think we're missing something,' Lalitha said.

Snow-white brought a tray with four cups of beverage. 'Tea,' she says. Everyone except Lalitha picks up the cups. Lalitha is not a tea person. Snow-white takes the left out cup and parks herself on the linen sofa facing the crowd peering over the screen.

Lalitha asks Siddha Goud to run the video from 8 p.m. to 8:30 p.m. She is watching the video alone as the others are busy sipping tea. Suddenly she slumps into a chair from the craning position.

It's as though Lalitha's muscles have suddenly decided to flee the town. Her legs give away. When she looks up again, her eyes are tinged red.

'Did you notice what I noticed?'

'What was that?' asks Venkat

'Roll the image left and right till about 15mins. A red SUV will go fast after the bike leaves the camera screen. And then after a minute or so, the same car returns in the opposite direction.'

'So what do you want me to conclude?' asks Venkatraman.

'The car resembles the one I had seen parked opposite our house a couple of months back – it was there for about four to five days. I noticed a familiar figure near the car looking at our house.'

'It could be a coincidence.'

But stranger things have happened.

Venkat has no answer – partly because he is not sure her supposition is accurate. He nods and lets her alone with her ghosts.

What is most troubling to me is the red SUV, the same car, parked in front of my house for about four days, about a month before the accident. I have to convince Venkat and the Police to investigate.

'Could you please rerun the film,' Lalitha requests the elderly gentleman.

It is now confirmed that the red SUV zooms past quickly – the timing matching with the time of the accident – and returns at double speed.

'Can you please freeze the frame when the SUV is visible, just to check the number plate,' requests Lalitha.

The camera is undoubtedly state-of-art; they could zoom to magnify enough to see the number plate. They had a partial vision when the car was going in one direction, and when it came back, the other part became visible, making it a complete picture. Lalitha asks Veeranna to note down the number.

Lalitha is now convinced that this SUV hit the bike on which her daughter was pillion, and the driver panicked and turned back and drove away. She says so to Venkat. She reaches out and takes his hand. Her flesh is cold and hard. 'All I'm asking is that you look closer.'

He had never seen such a pleading Lalitha in his entire life with her.

He tells her he will think about it. He tells her he will try to figure out the connection.

Venkat gets into the act. He dials Manjunatha, explains the entire scenario, and requests him to check the name of the owner of the vehicle and other particulars as available.

'Okay,' Manjunatha said, 'I will let you know.'

'Great. Then let's stay in touch, Inspector.' He cuts the phone.

The couple then profusely thanked Siddha Goud and requested a video copy. They exchange email ids.

Lalitha and Venkat, accompanied by a tired Veeranna, move to the accident site.

As they walk, they note that the road shrinks into a two-lane one from a three-lane main. Sensing the surprise on Venkat's face, Veeranna explains.

'The park on the left was much smaller than it is now. The locals wanted a walking path along the park's periphery and petitioned the local councillor. For future vote-bank quid-pro-quo, the councillor managed to get the sanction. The municipality encroached on the street because there was no space to expand to accommodate the park extension. This resulted in reducing the width of this road.'

'The biker may not have noticed this abrupt width reduction of the street on the dark rainy night, and also we gathered that the man was not a regular bike user, so he was not familiar with the roads around, even though he lived nearby,' adds Veeranna.

As they explore the site, they find construction debris that has not yet been removed. *Or maybe it's a new heap.* They look around and find a five-storeyed apartment – Swagath Ladies Hostel opposite the site of the accident. Every floor of the building facing the road has a balcony. Lalitha wonders whether anyone has seen the accident from the balcony. But then she realised that it was night and raining heavily. No one would venture into the balcony.

At the other end of the street, a pani-puri-wallah has a brisk business. A group of young women crowd him and gulp everything he serves. Traffic is whizzing past—a busy intersection.

Venkat notices a very pensive Lalitha. He is worried for her. Lalitha is deep in thought. An awful gurgling noise shoots out of her lips as though she is choking on some stems of a drumstick.

I careered around the pavement and recreated the incident described by the cop. I suddenly felt I want to hit someone, shout at someone, kill someone. I want to punch someone in the face. I want to stab someone through the heart. I want to do all that. I want to do all that.

Venkat takes her arm and leads her out. She follows him like a lamb. He calls for his driver as they wait at the site to return.

Venkat's mobile beeps.

'Sir, the Inquiry report has been submitted to the Government,' says his assistant engineer.

'So what happens now?'

'We have to wait for the action by the Government.'

'Who is that?' asks Lalitha

'Some office matter,' Venkat says. 'Subbaih, first drop me at the office and then you can take madam home.'

While in the car, Lalitha says, 'It gnaws at you. All day and night for over twenty years. It never stops. It never goes away. I have no control over what my mind is thinking. I am sorry about how I reacted to the video and at the accident place.'

Silence. Venkat has no idea what to say. But the silence was so thick he could hardly breathe. 'I am sorry,' he says.

She didn't look up. 'We shall go to the police and tell them about the video,' she says.

'What good will that do?'

'They'll investigate.'

'They already have. They think it is an accident.'

'But this new evidence should be brought to their notice. Veeranna will also corroborate.'

'I hope they will take it seriously enough to warrant a re-investigation,' Venkat says and gets down at his office and walks out briskly.

His mind is too confused with so many things happening around his life: Lalitha's presumptuous doubts, Shepherd's death and Kaveri in a coma in a hospital. What man can handle all at one time?

Chapter 16

'While you have been sitting there dreaming, I've eaten all the curry,' says Lalitha. She perches herself against the wall holding the dinner plate, and tries to seek Venkat's attention.

'Sorry,' says Venkat, mixing sambar and rice to make a gulpable morsel. He thought he was hungry, but his appetite, so erratic of late, has chosen again to disappear. It is difficult to explain the turmoil his mind is going through. Whatever he may say would be seen as an explanation of his grave error, and she would make it look like an irresponsible act that he should have been more careful about. Sermons, sermons. He is fed up with sermons. *She might read it in the newspapers, though. Doubtful. She is more of a "The Hindu" person; unlikely to read Bengaluru Chronicle – a tabloid. There are two reasons not to tell the truth – lying will keep someone from getting hurt, and lying will get you what you want – peace, mostly.*

Venkat is about to leave for his office when he receives a call from an unknown number. He reluctantly picks it up.

'Am I speaking to Mr Subramanian Venkatraman?'

'Yes.'

'I am calling from the chambers of the Secretary, Power. He asked me to request you to attend a meeting today at 11:00 a.m. at his Sachivalaya office.'

'Okay. I shall be there,' wondering what it is about.

Venkat skips his office and goes directly to the Office of the Secretary. He is about to enter Secretary's chambers, and the attendant at the door directs him to a conference room at the end of the corridor.

He is the first to enter the room. He finds a man of forty, bald and greying, placing folders in front of all the chairs. The chairs have no nameplates. So one can sit anywhere. The man recognises Venkatraman and greets and introduces himself as the Personal Assistant to Secretary. They exchange pleasantries. Venkat wants to ask what the meeting is about but decides not to.

Slowly the room gets filled up. Venkat can see his Executive Engineer, CE, MD and other staff of the Power Corporation coming in. They all greet each other. He finds a few more people in the room with whom he is unfamiliar.

The PA requests the members to pick up their coffees from the vending machine at the corner of the room.

As they sat, the PA said, 'Sir will join you in a few minutes. He requested you read the contents of the folder in front of you. If anyone did not receive the folder, please ask for it.'

Venkat opens his folder. The opening page is a photocopy of a news report.

POWER CORPORATION IS CORRUPT AND INEFFICIENT

By our Special Correspondent.

As the readers are aware, we had reported the callousness by which the Power engineers have dealt with the death of a poor farmer's son in a substation under construction at Thimmalahalli. Our investigations have led us to believe that the Power Corporation is very much responsible for this death because of their negligent handling of the contract. The Officers, however, made the contractor responsible for the poor fencing, which was the leading cause, as per their explanation in the press meeting held at the panchayat office of Thimmalahalli.

Our investigations have revealed that the contract was given to a contractor with little experience in the design and erection of substations. His experience was limited to some building and commercial complex electrical panel installations. Our sources inform us that some of the officers and engineers have tampered with the tendering process and awarded the contractor to this inexperienced contractor. The opposition MLA demanded an inquiry into the entire episode and insisted that the responsible engineers and officers be made accountable.

Await more information on the matter, as we have some more incriminating documents that will expose all that is happening in the Corporation.

The other papers in the folder contained the prelim report made by the site engineer immediately after the incident and his analysis of how it happened.

Meanwhile, the Secretary, a man in his fifties smartly dressed in a Peter England plain mustard-coloured shirt tucked in, enters the room, and everyone rises in acknowledgement of his rank.

Venkat notes the absence of the Chairman of the Corporation in the room.

The Secretary addresses, 'Good morning all. I am sorry that I have to assemble you on short notice of two hours. You will understand once I explain to you the gravity of the matter. I hope you have read the contents in the folder given to you. I am not here to seek any explanation. I am an IAS officer and not a technocrat. Please don't bombard me with technical jargon to confuse me. Whether what is written in the tabloid is truthful or otherwise is not the question in front of us. A milder version of this so-called investigative report also appeared in one of the leading newspapers, which gives credence to what is said in the tabloid. I am under pressure from the Minister since morning to go deep into the matter and explain to him so that he can call for a press conference and undo the damage done. I want the MD to give me a small gist of his departmental investigation in plain English so we can all sit together and solve the matter.'

Venkat notices that Sethuramaiah is taken aback by the sudden focus on him. He gets up from his chair and un-creases his upper garment, and addresses facing the Secretary.

'Thank you. Firstly, there is no compromise in the tender process. It is done exactly as per CVC rules. Even if CAG audits now, they will find no distortion, as this report claims. However, there were some lapses in the supervision of the construction. Firstly the fence design needed to have taken into account the soil strength. I want to avoid going into engineering details of the same. We have internally ordered a thorough revision of such boundary designs for future estates of the Corporation. Secondly, one particular earthing connection was compromised. Had this been in order, this unfortunate accident would not have happened. Even if a man or an animal went into the substation through the collapsed fence, the death would not have occurred if the grounding system had been installed and tested as per norms. We have failed in supervision before commissioning.'

The Secretary makes Venkat go over the total incident as per his reading of the site visit again in greater detail. Venkat frequently pauses to go over his story again so that as few technical terms are used as possible in deference to the opening statement made by the Secretary.

Of all the members present, only Venkat, CE and MD are aware of the circumstances of the change in the tender contractor from L1 to L2. One other person, i.e. Aravind Varma, who also knows the background, is not invited to this meeting today. None raised the matter of this issue. The person responsible for this change in the contractor, the Chairman, is conspicuous by his absence.

Now the Secretary takes charge.

'From what I know, I note that 1) there is a lapse in the drafting of the specification for the Fence, and 2) supervision of earthing was poor. As per the Karnataka Civil Services rules, every Government servant holding a supervisory post shall take all possible steps to ensure the integrity and devotion to duty of all government servants for the time being under his control and authority. Thus SE and EE become responsible for all the acts of his subordinates –i.e. Dy. EE & AE. This is my reading of the rules. However, we can't put someone in the dock without a proper inquiry. So, I shall recommend that the Minister establish a Disciplinary Committee per the Service rules and inform the press about it. We shall take from thereon.'

So announcing the Secretary left the room.

* * *

Next day, while Venkat is in a meeting with some of his colleagues at his office to discuss the aftermath of the discussion with the Secretary, an attendant from the Tappal office arrives, hands over a sealed envelope, and obtains his signature of receipt. The attendant also discovers that two other members to whom he has to deliver the mail are also in the room and hands over the letters to them.

All three open the letter to find an almost similar memo.

You......... are required to attend the first briefing of the Disciplinary Committee established under rule no......as per Karnataka Civil Services rules, at the Durbar Hall in the Secretarial premises on...... This is a charge under Rule 11 of the Karnataka Civil Services Rules.

The memo also contains information on the procedure to be adopted by the Commission conducting the inquiry.

You are invited to the proceedings of this Committee not only as an accused but also to record your statement as a witness of the actions that led to the unfortunate incident this Committee is investigating.

We have noted three acts of misconduct and dereliction of duty, which involves the entire hierarchy from the Superintending Engineer (Projects) down to the Assistant Engineer (projects). Hence a common charge sheet is being framed. However, the first act involving the issuance of the Tender Contract itself will be taken by the representatives of the Government at an appropriate time. This inquiry is limited to only design and erection-related issues at the site, as noted in the Terms of Reference.

* * *

Though Durbar Hall does not reflect a courtroom atmosphere, its setting isn't very comforting. The Commission members occupy the oak-panelled hall on a raised platform. The presiding chairman, Mr Parmananda, retired Chief Engineer, Andhra Pradesh Electricity Board, is flanked by two other members, Mr Alphonso Bevin, retired MD, Bengaluru Water Board and Mr Shankara Sastry, Retired Chief Engineer, Central Electricity Authority. Venkatraman, the SE; Gopal Krishnamurthy, the EE and Kapil Reddy, the AE, are occupying the chairs assigned to them with their respective name panels in front of them facing the platform on the ground level. An attendant is available to help with water and coffee; move papers from one table to another.

Parmananda states the purpose of the inquiry and says, 'We have placed the terms of reference of this Committee in the folder before you. We have substantial oral and documentary evidence already available, and there is no need to undertake any preliminary enquiry. So we are going ahead with the final submissions from you.'

'If any of you have any objections to these proceedings – the methodology and the terms of reference, please feel free to state, and it will be recorded,' adds Alphonso.

'There are two issues referred to us: 1. Fencing design and erection and 2. Earthing. We will seek your explanation on what went wrong at the site and advice on how we can avoid such lapses in the future,' said Sastry.

Sastry addresses no one in particular and asks for elucidation of the Border Fence installed at the site and where the Corporation had gone wrong.

'The Fence posts were directly embedded in the soil and backfilled with concrete around the pole. The concrete strength was checked for maximum compressive strength and found to be okay. The concrete was well-rodded in the hole. The top of the footing was crowned too,' explained the Executive Engineer, Gopal Krishna.

'We have ensured warning signs outside the Fence so that anyone who tries to trespass will be personally accountable and liable for the mistake. Our design norm requires the Fence for substations to have at least three strands of barbed wire, with a height of no less than seven feet. The boundary at Thimmalahalli is constructed precisely per the tender specifications,' added Kapil.

'Then why did the fence collapse?' Asked Parmananda, addressing Venkat.

'There was a dense rain accompanied by a heavy gale the previous night, which loosened the soil around some of the poles. This loose soil sunk two consecutive poles along with their concrete cylinder grips, and they bent at 45deg in opposite directions, leaving a significant gap in the barbed wire.' Venkat strives to keep his tone informal and calm.

'Who made these specifications? Are there any national or international specifications for the Fence?' asks Alphonso.

'The Fence specifications stay mostly the same across the country. It is a simple document. We have taken our specs from Uttar Gujarat Vij Company Ltd – UGVCL – a state government utility. A copy of these specs, part of the tender, is attached to the documents submitted to you. You may note the spec lists the MS posts and Chain link details and not anything on the civil erection part of the Fence itself. It is left to the site engineer for his insight and experience to guide the contractor. We have been installing fences at all our substations per the same specification as that used in Thimmalahalli. It is an unfortunate Act of God which resulted in the fence collapse.'

'You cannot give it up as an Act of God,' Shankara Sastry said, his irritation showing. 'What are you doing to ensure that it is not repeated?'

'We have discussed the matter with all the engineers and consulted the civil department of Bengaluru University. And now we are redrawing the Fence Specs so that such breakages don't occur.' Explained Gopala Krishna.

'Can I add to what Sir has said?' butts in Kapil.

'Yes, go ahead,' says Alphonso.

'Sir, let me read the relevant sentence in the spec of GVCL regarding the Fence: Minimum 450mm length of vertical posts should remain in the ground & it should be fixed up by the foundation of standard CC mixture of ratio 1:3:6 for the area of 300mm x 300mm & height of 475mm. There is no requirement to measure the strength of the ground itself, whether it can withstand nature's fury. It is left to the Site Engineer to ensure the poles are strongly embedded. We have installed the poles into the ground as per the practice followed in all our substations erections. This is the first instance of barbed wire fence breakage. However, with this experience, we are revising the Fence specs.'

'Can you explain briefly what changes you are proposing to make in the next such installations?' asks Sastry.

'We redesigned the base on which the fence would be standing in future. Raised kerb of concrete on the ground becomes essential when the soil strength is not enough. The kerb is made first by making a channel in the soil. This channel is lined with wood panels to ensure collapsing. The channel will also ensure a plumb line for the kerb. This is the bracing technique to prevent the side wall from collapsing. The wood panels are painted to prevent termite attacks. The galvanised poles are placed at the designed level before the concrete is poured. Thus the possibility of the entire concrete kerb sinking is almost nil. The fence wire shall be strung along the galvanised steel poles inserted inside the kerb,' explained Venkat.

'How are you ensuring that this new standard is always a part of the new contracts?' asks Parmananda. He returns his attention to Gopala Krishna.

'Sir, we have already sent this new specification to the Civil Engineering department of Bengaluru University to check and approve. As soon as the same is received, we shall inform the tender Committee,' assures Gopala Krishna.

During a short recess, Shankara Sastry corners Venkat and asks his opinion on the experience of the contractor who was given the job. Venkat has to tread carefully here.

'The L1 tenderer had yet to respond to our call for final negotiations and signing of the contract on the ground that his offer validity is expired. We tried to reason with him. Then we had to go to L2; as per CVC guidelines, we had to ask him to match the price of L1, which he did. Everything was above board. My EE and AE are sincere and are vastly experienced in supervising such electrical contracts.'

Venkat remains silent on the background of the Contract award, the Chairman's request and Venkat's subsequent meetings with Raman Rao and Bhruha of L1 to withdraw the offer, so L2 is given the contract as per the wish of the Minister.

Taking blame unfairly could be considered part of an assistant job.

The members assembled again after recess.

'It is reported in the investigation report you have presented that even if the fence allowed the unauthorised entry of the persons or faunae, the substation has enough safety precautions to prevent unintended electric shocks. Please explain what has gone wrong in this instance,' asks Parmananda.

Gopala Krishna says, 'Let me first explain earthing. To connect the metallic parts of electric machinery and devices to the earth, buried in the moisture earth, through a thick, low resistance conductor wire or plate for safety purposes is known as *Earthing or grounding*. Improper earthing allows the electric leak to flow back to the equipment and may cause damage to the equipment. While designing the earthing, equipment safety is the main focus; the intruder aspect is presumed to be nil because of security systems, warning signs and fool-proof Fences. However, this earthing also ensures the safety of the personnel operating the substation in case of an unintended leak, which may occur because of insulation failure.'

Venkat finds his mobile vibrating. It is Inspector Manjunatha on the line.

Venkat raises his hand and says, 'Excuse me, Sir, I have to take this call, which is urgent.'

Venkatraman had earlier approached the Chairman of the Commission at the start of the proceedings that he needed his mobile to be on the premises, albeit in silent mode, as his daughter is in a coma and he has to be ready to take any decision. For which the Committee agreed as a special gesture.

Venkat goes out to take the call and returns in a pensive mood after ten minutes.

The proceedings are kept pending till Venkat resumes his position.

'The report given to us shows that it was observed that the transformer core test stud and grounding link had melted, and displacement of LV windings was observed. What does that mean?' asks Alphonso.

'The grounding system usually consists of a grounding conductor that bonds the equipment to the ground. Earthing can be said to be the connection of the neutral point of a power supply system to the earth to avoid or minimise danger during the discharge of electrical energy. Usually, a copper strip bolted to the equipment body is connected to the earth grid. Earth faults occur when electricity 'escapes the wires' and returns to a substation through the ground. In this case, the electricity went through the body of the shepherd, which proved fatal,' said Gopala Krishna.

'Are there no preventive measurements possible for finding such leaks?'

'Yes, we do measure. A meter specially designed for measuring leakage currents is used. The current flowing in the ground conductor is measured by connecting the meter in series with the grounding connection. In this case, they were measured per the norms and records were submitted in the folder presented to the Government. We quantify the leakage current and then identify the source using Earth Leakage Relay (ELR),' said Gopala Krishna.

'You have not explained why this accident has occurred despite such elaborate test procedures. You are only presenting an ideal picture, and as per the incident, these procedures have not been followed. Please explain without beating the bush what and who is responsible for the current leak.' It is Shankara Sastry raising his voice in octave.

'Sir, a flat copper strip used to connect the transformer to the earth grid is found broken. When investigated, it was found that the strip used for connecting the transformer stud to the ground is not a single contiguous strip, but two stripes welded, probably to use up leftover copper strips. You know copper is an expensive metal. This weld gave away, and the copper strip broke at the weld joint, leaving the leakage current not grounded. When the shepherd touched the transformer, as he seemed to have tripped while walking around the substation in search of his sheep, he got electrocuted.'

'Mr Venkat, is this also an Act of God?' Parmananda asked sarcastically.

'When we measured the leakage current at all places, it was found to be as per norms. We overlooked this aspect of the contractor compromising on the copper strip connection. In a big substation, it isn't easy to keep physical track of every connection. We have to depend on the integrity of the contractor too. We do the leakage testing to ensure grounding is as per specs.'

'What action have you taken on the Contractor?'

'Sir, firstly, the compensation amount paid to the relatives of the shepherd is being recovered from the pending bills of the contractor. Secondly, we have sent a notice to him about why we should not debar him from participating in future tenders of the Corporation. Thirdly, we have asked him to recheck every earth connection in the presence of our AE and take corrective action. Also, he is asked to redo the fence as per the new norms. The last one re-erecting the fence, can be tricky as he has erected it as per the tender specifications. Departmentally we decided to take up the task of installing a new Fence,' said Venkatraman.

'Thanks for your cooperation. The recording of these proceedings is available with the Commission's secretary. If you want to deny or dispute anything said by you in the inquiry meeting or make new submissions in defence of the charge, you may want to do so within two days directly to the Commission Chairman. You need not go through your normal hierarchal route, and it will not be considered insubordination as an exception. We shall submit our findings to the Government within a fortnight,' says the Chairman.

Mr Alphonso stands up and says,' I request you to go through the case of one K Seetharam Bhat, an employee of KPTCL, vs the Disciplinary Committee Report of KTPCL. A young boy of 7 years had died because of the negligence of Mr Bhat. His one increment was held, and even though he approached the High Court later, his case was dismissed. I am quoting this to inform you that Bengaluru Power Corporation may also follow the same route while deciding on the penalty.'

The Committee rises for the day and disperses the members.

Chapter 17

The following morning, Lalitha awakes from the oppressive heat of a disturbing dream, and she tries to open her eyes but can't. She is in a courthouse; the ceiling fan in the courtroom is whirring with a creaky sound. The judge's gavel is thumped, and she is given a sentence – six months of simple imprisonment for misleading the court. She sits upright now and catches her breath. She finds Venkat's bed empty. *He has gone for a walk.*

She goes into the kitchen and puts the kettle on. The TATA coffee powder container is taken out, and she rams the powder into a percolator. After the water boils, she pours the water into the coffee maker.

As she sips her coffee at the dining table, Venkat walks in.

'The coffee is ready. Freshen up, and I will heat it up for you,' Lalitha says.

Venkat removes his sneakers and goes to the washroom. As he comes out, Lalitha asks, 'Any news from Manjunatha?'

'He called me, but I couldn't take the call as I was busy in a meeting. He sent me a WhatsApp message.' He lies. His mobile text notification ticks.

Venkat opens his mobile, reads the text and shows Lalitha the text.

The red SUV make Hyundai, registration number KA04 MB 4368, is registered to Karthik Enniguntla s/o Sheshadri Enniguntla, r/o H NO: 352/14, 7th main, 4th cross, Malleshwaram.

'So my hunch was correct.'

In ignoring her comment, Venkat says, 'we need to take a call on the matter after taking Manjunatha's advice.'

'Incidentally, what's news from the hospital?' asks Venkat.

'I spoke to Dr Vardhan. He said that there was no improvement in the GCS. But the baby is growing well. He sent the ultrasound image to my WhatsApp number. The image is a bit blurred because of the pixel differences between his gadget and mine. I could infer from the image that it could be a boy, though the doctor does not disclose the gender,' says Lalitha.

The couple reconciled to the fact that they would have an unwed mother in their family.

'Let me call Manjunatha.' Venkat punches the number on his mobile.

'Good morning, Inspector. I am sorry to disturb you so early in the morning.'

'It's alright. I am actually at the PS. I was on night bandobast and am about to leave for home now. Tell me, what is it?'

Lalitha signals Venkat to place the phone on speaker mode.

'My wife confirms that Karthik is the person who stalked her during her school and college days, and there is good evidence that this accident is not as it seems. She thinks it's some revenge on her.'

'Yes, Veeranna updated me on the matter. But I don't understand this revenge angle.'

'We can explain when we meet.'

'Okay, if you are so sure with your evidence, I suggest you file an FIR, and we can take the case from there on.'

'When can I come to meet you?'

'I suggest your wife file the FIR as she is the one who recognised the alleged perpetrator,' suggests Manjunatha.

'Okay, as you wish.'

'You can come with your wife after your office time, and then we can take it from there.'

'Thanks.' Manjunatha cuts the phone.

* * *

'Are you sure you want to go ahead with filing the FIR?' asks Venkat while dipping his idly in the sambar.

'You won't be able to stop me from committing errors of every kind. Let me make one error if you think filing the FIR was a mistake. One final time. After this, I'll abide by all your advice,' says Lalitha.

'You worry all the time. You spend so much time worrying that you barely ever live. Despite your busy schedule and dance commitments, you've fulfilled all your domestic duties. A terrific job. I didn't contribute anything besides caring for Kaveri during her formative years. I became too engrossed in my work to share your worries, concerns, and anxieties.'

'You have no idea how upset I am by the video and the thought of that rascal constantly monitoring me from his SUV. You can't deny that to me if I think he was involved in the accident.'

'Okay, as you wish,' and Venkat adds, 'Alright, let's do this. You come directly from your dance class to the PS. I will join you there. I will reconfirm the appointment after I speak to the inspector after my office hours.'

He rises to leave for his office.

* * *

'Are you sure that the person you saw in front of your house and the man seen on the video are the same?' asks Manjunatha.

Lalitha and Venkat are sitting in the PS in Manjunatha's chambers. Lalitha explained all the incidents involving her and Karthik during her college days.

'Yes,' says Lalitha.

'Based on what you have told me, we can connect the youthful Karthik who teased you in college to the middle-aged Karthik we saw in the video. That's simple. The fact that he was trying to stalk you after over twenty years is not supported by any evidence, though.'

'I swear I have seen him,' reconfirms Lalitha vehemently.

Manjunatha looks at Venkat for a cue. Venkat ignores and pretends to be reading his mobile messages.

'Do you have details of the court case you or your parents filed against him when he physically assaulted you?' asks Manjunatha.

'My appa may have. But he is now old. I don't want to trouble him with these matters. But it must be in the records of Malleshwaram PS.'

'I doubt we can get those details after so many years. In those days, there were no computers and hard discs to keep the records as we have today.'

'Okay, let me think. I need to get the opinion of my SHO. Meanwhile, you sit with Veeranna and draft the FIR. We shall decide on filing the same after a couple of days,' Manjunatha adds.

When they reach the car, Venkat notices a message on his WhatsApp from Manjunatha.

I need to talk to you alone, not in the presence of your wife. We will also consult with our SHO. I will fix a time and let you know.

Okay.

'I haven't cooked. Let's eat something in a restaurant,' Lalitha says.

The couple walks towards a nearby Nandini Food and Chat house, as recommended by Manjunatha. She stumbles on uneven pavement, but Venkat keeps her upright. They walk up the steps into a room with heat and humidity.

'Don't they have an AC room?'

Seeing the couple's uncomfortable posture, a man with an apron directs them upstairs.

They pick up their menus and order, but later neither of them can remember what they ate. Each one remembered their own apprehensions of the gist of their meetings with the police.

'I am totally confused over what to say and do,' Lalitha said, 'we need to discuss the issues raised by the inspector.' Venkat does not answer and vows to himself to keep the contents of the message that Manjunatha sent.

* * *

On the recommendation of his SHO, Manjunatha accompanies Venkatraman to meet the Deputy Commissioner of Police (north) – Mr Vasant Patil, to discuss the matter further and seek his guidance.

His office looks exactly as Venkat pictured; on the third floor of a building marked Police Head Quarters; at the end of a hallway lined with tables with computer screens, half of them unmanned; through two doors with ornate handles and a sentry to keep out the riffraff.

When the security guard notices the inspector in uniform, he opens the door. Manjunatha salutes his boss as per protocol. The Dy. C does not look up from whatever he is writing but acknowledges the salute with a wave of the hand. His shirtsleeves are rolled up—unusual for a man in uniform.

He stops writing and looks up. After introducing Venkat, Manjunatha tells Vasant Patil what the meeting is for, a short history of the case, and what Lalitha's crazy claim was. He places the police dairy report copy on his boss's table.

'Were there any eyewitnesses to the accident?' asks Patil.

'A maid who works in a ladies' hostel seems to have noticed the accident. Our HC had observed her on the balcony watching the ambulance removing the bodies. The witness was not lucid enough to rely upon. She had come to the balcony to remove the garments from the clothes hanger to avoid rainwater splashing all over the dried clothes. She heard some sounds below and happened to look down. She said the car, which we later learnt belonged to one Vivek, coming from the perpendicular lane, skidded too. She was unsure whether the car had hit the motorcycle, making the bike fall. We checked Vivek's version in detail. The motorcycle slipped because of the rain and slithered sand on the road and hit his car's right fender. He applied the break immediately, and his car must have veered around a bit. He was the one who called the police and the Ambulance.'

'And at another time, when the maid was called to the police station when her husband accompanied her, she said the bike skidded first and hit the stationary car. She is an unreliable witness. Interestingly, she does not seem to have noticed the lady who fell a little distance from her balcony. She thought that the bike had only one rider. A tree branch might have obstructed her vision to see across the street,' added Manjunatha.

'You referred to a red SUV, which was on the way to the accident site just before the accident, which your staff noticed in a private surveillance camera of a nearby household. And from your information, the vehicle belongs to one Mr Kartik, who Mrs Venkatraman believes could be an alleged perpetrator of either negligent driving or a thoughtful attack. Am I correct?' asked Patil.

'Yes, sir.'

'Have you done any further investigation into the matter?'

'Sir, as you know, we have not yet registered an FIR, without which I am not required to investigate. We are arranging this meeting with you on the advice of my SHO because we want your opinion on the FIR. However, my head constable checked whether the SUV vehicle had any tell-tale damage by visiting the Hyundai service stations around the city. It was negative.'

'Did the maid report seeing this SUV?'

'Sir, we have come to know of this matter of SUV only recently. We have not checked with the maid about this new information. However, she did not report seeing any car other than that belonging to Vivek, which we had thoroughly investigated and ruled out the possibility of negligence by Vivek.'

'And Mrs Venkatraman believes that the driver of the SUV is the same person who was earlier involved in stalking her and causing injuries to her,' says Patil.

'Yes, sir. That was almost twenty years ago.'

Mr Patil turns to Venkatraman and addresses him.

'Venkatraman sir, we both belong to the same government bureaucratic cadre. You rank higher than me by two levels in the hierarchy. I request you to listen to what I am saying with an open mind and let us reach a mutual consensus.'

'Alright, Patil, please.'

'The charge made by Mrs Venkatraman is a serious cognisable offence. As I see the report in front of me, she says the SUV driver may have hit the vehicle by negligent driving, or he may have pre-planned to attack the motorcycle with a motive to kill. There is no witness to the incident, so we don't have enough evidence to say that the vehicle hit the bike. But it is still a matter of investigation. An FIR is a written document prepared by the police when they receive information about the commission of a cognisable offence, after which an investigation is carried out. A charge sheet is a formal document of accusation prepared by a law enforcement agency.'

'I understand.' I move slightly in the chair, uncomfortable about what he will say.

'If Mrs Venkatraman wants us to file an FIR on the charge of attempt to murder or cause grievous harm, we can't deny her the right. However, let me add a rider here. From what I have heard from Manjunatha, it could be a case of mistaken identity. The incident reported by the two constables at the mishap site indicates that it was purely an accident. And there was no sighting of any SUV other than the Swift my staff had recorded. Filing an FIR requires the investigation agencies and courts to expend valuable time. We don't want to add to the already crumbling judicial system unless we have a tight case. It is now for you to take a decision.'

I am in a bind. If I don't act as per Lalitha's insistence on revenge by the car owner, who is now identified as Karthik and the same person who stalked her and caused irreversible damage to her plans, I would need a more plausible reason than pending cases in courts. So I compromise.

If it was one thing that Venkat wanted to maintain at all times, it was peace with Lalitha, if not bonhomie.

'What if, without filing a formal FIR, the inspector calls the driver of the vehicle, interrogates him, and gets more details?' I ask.

'Many of my staff do that as an exigency. I don't recommend it in this case, as the person is the son of a prominent lawyer. We shall register an FIR, as per section 154 of Cr. Pc. However, instead of registering the offence under section 307—i.e., murder attempt—we shall register it under section 304A, the negligent act causing death. Manjunatha will do the needful. Because this is a cognisable offence, we need not inform the courts of an investigation that includes calling the alleged perpetrator of the offence to a police station for interrogation. However, I don't recommend arrest, though we would be right as per law to arrest him and then produce the accused before the courts.'

He then gets up from his chair, indicating that the meeting is over.

I say thanks and leave the office. I return to my office to close my unfinished business before returning home. I brief Lalitha on the matter. She listens quietly. On an audio phone, you don't have the advantage of observing the body language of the recipient's reaction. She says okay and hangs up.

* * *

My WhatsApp notification bell hums. My father has bombarded me with messages.

When are you going to learn, Maga? I've told you a million times not to answer police calls. You are the son of a lawyer. Act the part. Not like the average citizen, who is constantly afraid of the police. Why did you go to Sanjayanagara PS without telling me? Don't bother asking me how I know. There isn't a single police department in the world that is airtight.

I have a tough time retracting the statements you gave to the police. However, this PS has a tough police officer who goes by the name of Manjunatha. Not any run-of-the-mill guy. He thinks he is an incarnation of Satya Harischandra. A tough nut.

The last message gives me hope.

I understand there is an FIR, and they are investigating an accident in which you are named as a suspect. That is a serious accusation. They may file a charge sheet against you, and you may receive a summons. Meet me in my office after my court appearance this evening. Also, don't bring any of your girlfriends.

The last sentence is typical of my dad, reminding me I am a womaniser.

I would lash out if it weren't for my dad. But I need him more than he needs me. My entire business depends on his influence in political and bureaucratic circles. Out of everyone I could confide in, my dad isn't at the top of my list. It is easier to talk to someone who has no background information on you.

I reach his office at about 7 p.m. I see him pacing the floor and dictating to his secretary, Parvathi Shanbagh. I watch a mature lady, plump, with a dark complexion. She had a pencil in her ear and another in her hand, furiously scribbling in shorthand.

Maybe around forty. She covers her body with her pallu, and I can't picture her breast size.

She had long hair flowing to her forearm. My dad sees me and waves me to sit.

I pull up a chair next to her to watch her closely. She does not acknowledge my presence lest she misses a sound bite. She has been with my dad for over a decade now. Maybe longer. My dad once told me that she is the epitome of efficiency and that he can perform so well in court because she manages the office with an efficiency that would be envious of any corporate manager. My mother doubted her integrity, though. Parvathi helped my dad during my marriage too. Decoration, caterers, reception arrangements, the works. It annoyed my mother. This is purely a family function; why is she interfering?

Dad finishes his dictation, and the lady walks out with a slight limp. She has heavy buttocks and must be a mother of a dozen children, or her husband is fond of doggy style, or she is promiscuous. Looking at her visage, the last one is undoubtedly out of the question.

My dad starts his address to me without salutation, as though he is continuing where he left off while narrating the text for transcription.

'Whatever you've done is irreversible. But tell me honestly, were you involved in the unintentional death of a young man and a woman, which the police are looking into?'

'No,' I say.

'Good. Then explain the entire incident from the beginning.'

'Also, verbatim of the talk you had with the Inspector,' he adds.

I narrate as I recollect. I omit the vigil opposite Lalitha's house. I dragged Lalitha out from the pages of my memory. Every atom of her being.

The security guard asked for my credentials as I entered the police station. I gave it to him, and he led me to the inspector's chambers. The inspector had a couple of other visitors who were conversing with him. I drew a chair close to them and sat down. The inspector glared at me. How-dare-you-sit-without-permission. Kind of. After about 30 minutes, he looked at me and asked who I was. When told, he called his sub-inspector, Veeranna, to be present with his notebook.

'Name and address.'

I gave the details once again.

'Is KA04 MB 4368, the registration number of your vehicle—a red Hyundai SUV?'

'Yes.'

'Were you driving your Hyundai SUV on Sanjayanagara Main Road on Sunday, the 23rd of September?'

'Yes.' Veeranna was taking copious notes.

'Did you hit a biker on the road?'

'No.'

'Then why did you turn around from the accident scene?'

How did they come to know of this? I underestimated the intelligence and seriousness of the Bengaluru police!

'I found the road narrowed and was blocked by a car in an angled manner and a motorcycle lying flat, and I could not go forward, so I had to turn back.'

'Do you know this person?' The inspector thrusts a picture of a young girl towards me.

A replica of a young Lalitha. But Lalitha was much prettier at that age. I don't divulge this information to my dad, either.

'No,' I say.

'Do you know this person?' The inspector pushes another picture of a middle-aged lady.

I could recognise an older Lalitha. The one I saw climbing into her Santro. Very elegant.

'No.'

'The lady claims you were seen in front of her house for five days in a row last month, and she also recognised your SUV. What are your thoughts on that?'

That's news to me. What is Lalitha accusing me of? That I bumped her daughter off?

'I have no idea who she is or where she lives. So no question of going anywhere near her.'

'That's all, dad. The inspector asked me to leave after noting all the above and making me sign the transcript.'

'Did he not threaten you with arrest? According to the FIR, the death was caused by a negligent act, an offence under Section 304A of the IPC. The police have the authority to arrest you. I'm surprised he didn't.'

'I'll take care of it. Meanwhile, any police call or message should be reported to me immediately before you take action,' my dad adds.

Chapter 18

Laila Kutti, our favourite head nurse, stays late some nights just so that any slightest movement by Kaveri is recorded. The head nurse is a model of resolve and optimism on the surface, but I have seen her teary-eyed as she is sponge-bathing Kaveri. Kutti has become attached to my daughter. Also, she convinced the management to install a closed circuit camera in the ward, lest the night nurse's fatigue may miss out on any jerk or an eye-lid opening. Kaveri's employers paid for this arrangement, as there was no precedent in the hospital for such an arrangement.

The notification sound on Lalitha's mobile wakes her up. She sees the message, wakes me, and passes her mobile for me to read.

Kutti Head Nurse

Kaveri is kicking her legs. She opened her eyes once and closed them again. Please visit the hospital as soon as possible. I informed Dr Ingalhalikar too.

05:30

We hurry to the hospital after receiving a call from the ward personnel.

The doctors instructed us to wait outside the room while they examined the patient.

As all the doctors and their PG interns exit, Dr Ingalhalikar addresses Lalitha.

'I'm happy to let you know that your daughter's condition has significantly improved. She is reacting to stimuli slowly. We cannot distinguish the activity that the brain electrodes are exhibiting. We will keep an eye on things.'

'I'm grateful, Doctor. We'd like to see our daughter.'

'Sure,' says the doctor, 'after that, come to my cabin, and we'll talk further.'

He then departs with Dr Vardhan. Our daughter is still vegetative when we see her in bed, but this time she has electrodes inserted in her brain that are connected to a screen apart from other paraphernalia like a feed tube etc. Her baby bump is showing up now.

Kutti explains, 'When the doctor spoke to your daughter and said her name, you could see from her closed eyelids that her pupil moved a little. While Dr Ingalhalikar scratched her plantar aspect, the sole of her foot, there was a slight elbow movement.'

That provides us with some optimism.

'How is the infant?' Lalitha queries.

'Good. The foetus is developing just like any healthy lady's foetus would.'

We moved to the neurosurgeon's cabin as requested by him.

He is reading what appears to be a medical publication while holding a magnifying lens. He does not look up.

He motions for us to take a seat while keeping his eyes glued to the page in front of him. First, he stops reading. Then he lifts his head and addresses us as if he is delivering a lecture to his students.

'What is very frustrating for us neurosurgeons is unlike the other parts of the body, the brain can't self-repair. We have to keep working around it. The fundamental idea or philosophy in any activity, particularly in medicine, is the idea of hope. Without the correct prognosis and no optimism, nothing will be accomplished. I am experimenting with the methods employed since 2001 by a German physician with extensive expertise in reviving coma patients. The patient is spoken to with incorrect sentences – deliberately. The electrodes connected to the patient's brain activate in response to the patient's actions, shown on the CRT. This experiment shows that Kaveri's brain contains a window of consciousness. We also discovered that frequent physical therapy is beneficial. Both are being done. Your daughter fights well. I am sure it won't be long before your daughter goes into everyday life. As I told you, I cannot give you a timeline.'

'When was she admitted?' the Doctor inquires.

'On the 10th of February,' I say.

'It is already June now. She has been in a coma for close to four months. However, the improvement is heartening. You do not know their potential if we only test the patient clinically. So, I have a suggestion for you. A patient in a coma frequently interacts with medical professionals and other personnel unfamiliar to her. The presence of relatives with familiar voices can help to increase brain activity. This is what the German Doctor instructed, and he worked with his patients successfully. I advise one of you to remain in the room constantly and engage her in conversation. Tell her some ridiculous things first, check to see if anything is happening and update the attending nurses. I have faith that she will recover quickly.'

We say thanks and leave his room. We decided to stay put in her ward in turns – day and night. Lalitha during the day and I in the night.

* * *

Expenses at the hospital had never been a problem for us. Kaveri's office was generous not only with flowers and good wishes but with financial support.

On the third day of the accident, I eagerly awaited my morning coffee as I watched Lalitha come with two Styrofoam cups from the canteen. As I stand to get up to help her, I notice two gentlemen come towards me with folded hands in an Indian gesture of salutation. They are tall and in an office get-up; one a Caucasian and the other a North Indian (fair skin). The Caucasian speaks, 'I am Edward Faunton, an HR manager from the Singapore branch of the office where your daughter works, and this gentleman is Aravind Goel, Miss Kaveri's immediate superior here in Bengaluru. We are incredibly sorry about this sad crisis that has hit your family. Our company values Kaveri's employment and wants to assure you on behalf of the company that we shall help you tide over this emergency – both financially and emotionally. Please feel free to ask us anything you need.'

I Namaste them and thank them for their gesture. Lalitha, with both hands filled with coffee cups, nods, acknowledging what they say. I introduce Lalitha to them.

Aravind, addressing Lalitha, says, 'we have already informed the reception to send all the hospitalisation bills to us at the office address, and accordingly, we signed all the required documentation. Also, if you need to buy any medicines outside the supply stocks of this hospital, please let us know we shall arrange it.' He thrusts his visiting cards in our hands – one for each.

'Thanks for your kind offer. We are forever indebted to you,' says Lalitha.

The two gentlemen bow and walk out as though they are departing from a corporate meeting room after winning accolades.

I remember the date clearly – 14th July 2019. It was Lalitha's duty day, but being a Sunday, I took her shift.

I am watching Kaveri carefully for signs of consciousness. Ventilator with a trach tube. Vital signs monitor. Feeding tube. IV med dispenser. I checked out, and they worked fine.

I notice that her facial expressions change from time to time. She has dreams, I believe. There could be a possibility of resuscitation. I then notice her legs kicking. I am elated and ask the ward boy to call Kutti. As Kutti enters, she goes near the hearing distance of Kaveri and calls her name. There was a murmur. Unmistakably.

Kutti loudly sounds her name again and asks me also to call. I say in Tamil, 'Ponni, kamaniye edunzare[13].' My Ponni opens her eyes. Kutti is elated. She shouts at the ward boy to call the duty doctor, Dr Vardhan and Dr Ingalhalikar, on the PA system. I call Lalitha to rush to the hospital, giving very little information to avoid overexcitement and tension-driving. Being Sunday, my driver is not available.

Dr Vardhan is the first to arrive. He examines her and does all that is needed to ensure that she is responding to his stimulus. He pats her baby bump gently and smiles.

'You know Venkatraman, it is the baby that woke her up. The baby is seeking the mother's attention.

Fortunately for her well-being, her mind won't let her remember the tragic events that led to her present state.'

---

13. Ponni, wake up dear

'She had always been an outgoing child with strong social skills and quick to learn,' Venkat says optimistically.

* * *

'It's been nearly five weeks since your daughter started responding to stimuli. How is she doing now?' inquires Ambrish Varma.

Ambrish and Venkat are sitting in Venkatraman's office, sipping tea. It has been their routine for a long time. Their friendship is not limited to office matters. They confide in each other on personal issues too.

Venkatraman's office appears to be the work of a young Lee Kuan Yew[14]. A neat desk adorned by a computer with a wireless mouse; and one photo of his daughter, Kaveri, when she was a cute baby, placed facing him. There is one mug of water with a coaster to protect it from dust and bacteria.

They are currently sitting on a couch placed to entertain casual visitors in the corner of Venkat's room.

'Thank God, my daughter has almost completely recovered – 98%'

'I congratulate you and Lalitha. Your love and patience are largely responsible for Kaveri's quick recovery.'

'It's not only us. Everyone pitched in. The doctors, nurses, and Kaveri's colleagues too.'

'Do you mean office colleagues?'

---

14. Former PM of Singapore, known for his attention to detail and meticulous tending of the city's international image of being a "Garden City", something that has been sustained to this day.

'Yeah. As soon as we informed Kaveri's office of her improved condition, her boss, Mr Aravind, came to the ward and spent time with her. He was narrating some anecdote or another of his office gossip, even though she was not fully aware of him and his conversation. He also directed Kaveri's co-workers to visit and spend time with her. It was also the doctors' directive to us. "Keep talking to her," they advised.'

'That's nice,' Ambrish said as he dipped a Parle glucose biscuit into his tea.

'Even my driver, Subbaih, has contributed too. He used to drive her around town, showing places Kaveri used to frequent, as soon as we were told she needed to be taken around to familiarise herself with the surroundings.'

'How long will it take her to return to normalcy?'

'The hospital authorities have discharged her, and she is already home. She climbed the stairs to her first-floor room for the first time in about five months. We let her be on her own, as directed by the medical staff. I think it will take another week for her to communicate with us. Hopefully.'

'Did you bring up the subject of her pregnancy?'

'The doctors have forbidden us from discussing the matter until she raises it herself. Surprisingly, she is caring for herself in the same way that any other would-be mother would. She takes the medications given to her without complaint. Dr Vardhan, the Gynaecologist, has instructed us to feed her an iron-rich diet because she is anaemic. Kaveri is very cooperative in these matters,' Venkat explained.

'Miraculous. I have to say.'

'I believe her resilience helped us to survive this crisis more than anything else,' said Venkat.

Ambrish sees a tear run down Venkat's cheek, which he wipes away with the back of his hand.

* * *

At early dawn, Venkat and Lalitha are startled by a shriek from Kaveri's bedroom.

Kaveri is not permitted to sleep in her usual upstairs room because she has not recovered completely. Her parents put her up in Attaih's room downstairs, which had been vacant since Attaih died. They spruced up the room to look as close to Kaveri's original setup in her upstairs residence as possible. They moved a portion of her wardrobe, the Wi-Fi, and the laptop downstairs to reacquaint her with her authentic surroundings. This room is next to her parent's bedroom, allowing them to keep an eye on their daughter through the night.

They both jump out of bed, dash towards her room, push open her door, turn on the light, and rush in. Venkat grabs his daughter and clutches her tightly to calm her.

Kaveri, now fully awake, brushes her appa away and screams, 'Where is my phone?'

'We are here, dear. It is all right,' Venkat says, disregarding her phone matter. Lalitha straightens her dress and adjusts the blanket.

Her parents exchange glances.

'The battery in your phone is dead. I'll charge it right now,' assures Lalitha.

Snubbing her amma, Kaveri addresses her appa and says, 'Appa, I need my phone right now.'

'By the time you get freshened up, the phone will be charged,' assures Lalitha.

They lead her to the restroom and shut the door behind her.

'Why does she need her cell phone?' asks Lalitha.

'It is a good sign that she has almost recovered. Let her come for breakfast, then we may get more info,' Venkat calms his wife.

A hot case of idlis and a flask of coffee are on the breakfast table, along with upma and chutney. Kaveri comes to the table, neatly dressed as if she is about to leave for work.

Kaveri tells her parents about Athreya and her relationship with him at the breakfast table with the clarity of a mature woman. The couple is in a quandary – whether to be happy about her full memory recovery or feel muddled about what she just explained – about Athreya and their relationship.

'Before you use your mobile, we want you to take you to consult Dr Vardhan, who is your doctor.'

'What's my mobile got to do with the doctor?'

'That is the recommendation from the hospital. According to the doctors, sudden exposure to external information may be risky.'

Venkat's daughter, who trusts him to tell her when it's safe to cross the street, to tie her hair into two tiny plaits, and to protect her from all sorts of horrible things like large dogs and loud noises, stares at him and says, 'I want to talk to my friend. What is the risk in it? How can you or the doctors prevent me?'

Her parents notice a pained expression on her face. It bothers them. They are afraid of exposing her to the truth about Athreya, so a doctor's advice comes in handy to buy time.

Finally, Kaveri relents and returns to her idlis and coffee.

Venkat schedules a meeting with Dr Vardhan and Dr Ingalhalikar. He informs them about the situation ahead of time, so they can deal with her wish.

* * *

Kaveri pauses on the low steps of the hospital, looks at the signage, and then slowly walks behind her parents. When the neurology department's receptionist notices the visitors, she opens the door to the consultation room and lets them in.

Dr Vardhan sits in a chair next to Dr Ingalhalikar, and both extend their hands to welcome Kaveri and her parents. Kaveri nods, adjust her top and sits with her elbows on the table, her gaze intent, as if eager to learn about a new wonder.

'Congratulations, Kaveri. That is indeed a quick recovery. Your parents tell us that you have fully recovered your memory now. It's like having a second chance at life, a different one, but maybe a better one – who knows? '

'Thank you very much. But my parents do not want me to return to normalcy. They are overly protective of me, treating me like a child and denying me screen time.'

'That is not correct. Your parents went through a lot in the six months you've been in a coma. They want to ensure that your introduction to the outside world is gradual and not abrupt.'

'All right,' Kaveri shrugs and settles back into her chair, waiting for the doctor to elaborate.

Then Dr Vardhan inquires, 'how do you feel about your pregnancy? Are you happy?'

'Yes, of course. Which woman wouldn't be happy to be a mother? I am already sensing my baby's movements.'

Slowly but lucidly, Dr Ingalhalikar explains the accident and the demise of Athreya with as much detail as required as per their training in handling coma-recovered patients.

'Are you sure? Athreya is not alive?'

'Yes, I am afraid so,' says Dr Ingalhalikar.

'Do you mean he has been dead for almost six months?'

While everyone in the room waits for her to recover, she covers her face with her palms to wipe off her tears. Lalitha hugged her daughter without saying anything because the doctor told her to allow recovery to progress gradually. Also, such debilitating information must come solely from the doctors.

'I am carrying his child within me. And he has no idea. Unfair,' she says with a weepy voice.

Tears stream down her cheeks. Dr Vardhan gives Kaveri some tissues. Kaveri pushes her chair back, stands up, and looks up at the ceiling before sitting down. Venkat extends a glass of water to her, which she declines. Kaveri then does something completely unexpected. She gets up from her chair and rushes out of the room. Venkat is about to walk down the corridor toward Kaveri. Dr Ingalhalikar motions for him to refrain from following her and gestures to leave her alone for a while.

'How do you think this information affects my child?' Lalitha inquires.

Before the doctors respond, Venkat says, 'She's such a good girl. She's always done what we asked her to do.' Lalitha nods, unable to speak.

Venkat and Lalitha are not the first parents to face the dilemma of having an unwed mother, but they are the first to announce the death of a person responsible for their daughter's condition.

The doctors vacate the room to leave the parents alone to recover.

Venkat and Lalitha rise from their seats and walk into the corridor; they notice Kaveri on the chrome sofa next to a child playing with her doll while her amma is busy talking on her phone. Venkat sits next to his daughter and squeezes her hand; he feels a slight throb and lets her fingers interweave with his as she claws back into this world.

Kaveri recovers slightly. The three drive back to their home after taking further instructions from the doctors on her medication.

* * *

Here's my question: At what age do you accept that the person you loved the most is no longer with you? What are you doing in heaven, leaving me alone here? Do you feel the pain of separation as I do? The doctors said my baby is fine, and I can deliver a healthy child, but you aren't here to share the joy of parenthood. Yet, I am picturing you right now wishing me well. You promised to introduce me to your parents. You failed me, Athreya.

I request my appa to take me to Athreya's apartment.

At the dining table, appa informs amma about my wish. My amma's eyes move from my appa to me, 'What purpose will this visit achieve?' My appa ignores the question but insists on accompanying me. I accede to his request. I call Gaurinath and make an appointment to visit him.

We drive down to his Daffodils apartment, as both Gaurinath and Banerjee greet us; if they are surprised by my pregnancy, it is not visible in their expressions. I walk around the apartment and notice that nothing has changed much.

I ask Gauri, 'Can I see his room if it is not occupied by anyone else?'

'Sure, we have not yet found the right person to share the room. And we wanted to keep Athreya's memory a little longer,' said Gaurinath.

I walk into his room. My appa leaves me alone and doesn't follow me to the room. He wants me to relive my experience with Athreya in silence. He looked at me and nodded.

I just let my gaze down on Athreya's bed, where he once slept. A neat bed: covered with a white coloured with flower motif satin duvet. The balcony is closed. I open it to see pigeon poo all over the place. I immediately shut it. I turn to the room and picture myself in that bed, unfurling myself after that day's passionate lovemaking, running my fingers through his rough goatee. What, in the name of GOD, is my mind thinking of cots and beds at a time like this? When will it sink in that Athreya is no longer with me? But it isn't straightforward. I need him alive, require him to take me to his parent's home and say, "Amma, this is Kaveri, your future daughter-in-law."

I come to my senses and see the empty bed. I couldn't control myself and walked out quickly with moist eyes. I use the bathroom and return to the hall where Gaurinath and my appa are talking.

'Do you have his parents' address?' I ask Gauri.

'It took me four days to learn about the accident because I was away on a site visit. On police insistence, I hacked Athreya's laptop, noted his parents' phone number and address, and passed it on to the Inspector, Manju, or some such name. I have not stored the information anywhere else. Hoping it can be retrieved from his computer. One day, about a couple of months back, his parents took away all his belongings, including his laptop, so we have no information on his parents' whereabouts. I was not in town that day. The couple came with a police constable to our apartment. Banerjee was intimidated by their behaviour and did not bother about what they were taking away from Athreya's room, which belonged to him, anyway. We are wondering how to contact Athreya's father to discuss Athreya's share transfer. Kothari also wants to know the path forward for the company. So far, Ganesan is managing the client end with borrowed resources from Kothari's parent company. I have not been able to contribute much because of my work schedule pressures. Ganesan had made a ruckus at the hospital admin for the lack of diligence in keeping their records. It was futile. If you need help finding Athreya's parents' contact and address, we would gladly assist in our mutual interest.'

How are you running the company without Athreya? I want to ask.

I put it back for another day. I have no courage to talk to Gaurinath on any matter.

I say thanks. Appa and I leave the apartment.

I need something much more substantial than luck.

I rush out with appa and wait for the driver to enter the front gate. While waiting for it to arrive, I stand across the street, glance up, and stare at the apartment. A moment later, Gaurinath's face appears on the balcony, and he waves to us. I wave back. I notice that he is dabbing his eyes with a tissue. My plight as much moves him as did my parents. Athreya must be an excellent friend to drive a man to tears.

* * *

I take a sip of coffee, sitting on the upstairs room's balcony, ruminating over my state of mind. I could convince my parents to let me start using my upstairs room, at least during the daytime. But I have to sleep in attaih paati's room downstairs at night. My amma has not been running her dance school for the last six months. However, I am told that a few students come home to learn. But she is paying rent for the dance institute, which is now a well-established school, and my amma wants to maintain the locational advantage she gained over twenty years. I am still not clear in my mind when and how I will be able to convince my amma to restart her formal teaching routine by reopening the school.

I worry about my parent's concern about my unwed mother's status. I can't change the condition. Sometimes I hate myself for putting my folks in this situation. I can't push my memory away whenever it floods upon me. If I can establish contact with Athreya's parents, some legitimacy can be restored, so my parents can breathe easy. Today I shall convince my appa to take me to the Police Station to check their records for the address of Athreya's parents.

On amma's insistence, we let her accompany us to the police station.

'Your appa is always in the world of his office and electric shocks. He forgot how to hold hands when you grew up as an adult. I don't want you to slide on the uneven pavement blocks or at the entrance steps, as you are not stable enough to manoeuvre such slips. Such a fall can be dangerous for you and the child in you. I have to come with you.'

We had a prior appointment, so the security guard at the entrance immediately ushered us into Inspector's cabin. My appa held the double door open, and we walked in. A man of fortyish with a ragged look and unshaven beard with a square chin stands up from his chair and welcomes us with folded hands of Namaste. He speaks in Kannada about not giving us time earlier, but having noted our blank faces, he shifts to English.

We state our purpose.

'It rained heavily that night. We had many accidents involving bikes and cars. Some third-party claims had to be entertained, for which the insurer needed to file an FIR. Our staff were inundated with these requests. Yet, I took the responsibility of investigating the antecedents of the injured while a do-gooder who was present at the time of the accident helped by calling an ambulance and moving the injured to a private hospital.'

'Ramaiah Memorial Hospital had declared the person dead on arrival. In all such unidentified dead bodies, the police officials shall immediately contact the nearest Medical College/ CMHO/ Medical Jurist to collect viscera samples to preserve the same for DNA comparison/analysis as and when required. Also, to preserve the body in a mortuary as per norms. I could finally locate the father's phone numbers with the help of the deceased man's roommate; I called them up and asked them to come over urgently. They met me at the PS, and I accompanied them to the mortuary. During the journey, I remember that the mother introduced herself as Bhanumati. She was curt with me for the delay in informing them of the accident, and that's how I remember her name.'

'You know, my grandfather was a fan of a Telugu film heroin who also doubles as a singer, so he named my amma after her – Bhanumati.'

When Athreya said her name holding it in his mouth as if it were his favourite sweet dish, it sounded so different to me. I felt she meant a lot to him, I vaguely recollect.

'Do you have the telephone numbers of her or her husband?' my appa asks.

'I am afraid not. My mobile is full, and I don't save numbers I don't need anymore. The purpose was served when I led them to the hospital's morgue. They took it from there.'

His voice is almost flat, but I hear the regret more than his words. My brain is fizzling with possible ways to find Athreya's parents.

We take leave and walk in silence to the car.

While in the car, I clasp my hands together in a prayer gesture and say, addressing my amma, 'let us go to the mortuary; they may have the details.'

'I don't suggest you go to any hospital, that too to a morgue. I don't want to expose you to infection at this stage of your pregnancy. I forbid.' She was firm in her tone.

I look at my appa, 'Appa. Please?'

'I agree with your amma. It is not safe in that Government hospital.'

'But till recently, I was in a hospital environment,' I mockingly protest.

'Ponni, that was different. You were in a special ward, fully sterilised and monitored 24/7, thanks to the generosity of your employers. Don't compare that with a Government Hospital.'

'I can go alone and try,' adds my appa as a concession. My appa doesn't give any hints up front; he makes his move.

We agree, and he hires an Uber, leaves for the hospital, and Subbaih drives us back home.

* * *

Kaveri pulls the sheet over her body and stares dry-eyed at the ceiling, wondering when she will feel happy. She loved Athreya with sinking helplessness and craved his presence at all times. Providence has played dice with her; she came out short. Once she meets his parents and explains, everything may fall into place. Or will it? What will she tell Athreya's mother? Kaveri wasn't sure how much his mother knew about the changes in relationships in the contemporary world. Is it possible for her to imagine her son having physical relationships before marriage? Is she modern enough to understand her? Will she accept Kaveri's child as her son's? If she doesn't and slams the door, what then? There isn't anybody she can talk to. She has to figure it out for herself. Or maybe she can talk to her friend Susan.

She gets up, feeling shaky and picks up the bedspread from the floor and wraps it around her again. Losing her virginity before marriage is unusual in her society. Imagine if her amma was in the place of Athreya's mother, will she accept her child? She is not sure. Maybe she will. Lalitha is exposed to foreign cultures because of her frequent visits to the US.

When hearing Venkat's car's sound, Kaveri rushes to the door to open it before he rings the bell.

'What news, Appa?'

'No luck.'

Kaveri gazes at him. 'What does that mean?'

'It means that the morgue attendant does not have all details. I have seen the document signed by the parents while taking possession of the body as per the protocol. They have affixed their Aadhar[15] numbers below their signature as proof of address. I could not decipher the father's name from the signature. The

15. Identity card – the Indian equivalent of a US Social Security card

mother's signature was clear – Bhanumati,' Venkat says, 'when asked whether they had taken a copy of the Aadhar card for records, the incompetent clerk feigned ignorance. The male nurse at the morgue said they had scanned the copy and returned the original back to them. He was unable to locate the scanned image. We searched and also called the IT help desk but to no avail. The computer operator said another person had come wanting to know the addresses of his parents. He told me, "He was very curt with us, and we had literally thrown him out of the hospital and threatened to call the police". Obviously, he was referring to Ganesan.'

The morgue attendant couldn't retrieve the data with the most modern system he had. My appa informed me that the hospital clerk stored a scanned copy of the Aadhar information on their hard disc instead of manual input into their DBMS. The regular computer operator was on leave that day, and his reliever did not know how to use the DBMS. So, he simply scanned the Aadhar cards and stored them in the bulging computer belly. Apparently, the attendant had forgotten to inform the regular operator to enter this data into the database once he resumed duty. There was no standard operating procedure for retrieving such information. Also, there was no indication of which folder such records were kept in. My appa had to abandon his efforts after an hour of search with an uncooperative computer operator.

Fate surprises you when you least expect it.

'Can't we get the address from the Aadhar number?'

'General public doesn't have access to such information from UIDAI[16].'

16. Aadhar administration portal.

Kaveri felt a slight chill. She sat still, looking at her clasped hands. Her appa's words settled within her like goblets of mercury. Whatever it takes. Whatever has to be done. She has to find Athreya's parents' address and meet them in person.

I remember an old incident. When I was nine or ten and was allowed to ride the bike – only until the lane ended – I watched the sun go down in crimson red. I rode the bike faster, racing against the sunset to do as many rounds as possible. Sunset was the deadline given by my amma to return home. I kept on skipping the deadline, only to be reprimanded by amma. I find myself doing the same thing, bargaining with my parents to do my own thing before I deliver my baby.

Chapter 19

Tired and so hungry that my appetite had faded entirely away to be replaced by a deeper, gnawing unease, I changed into a housecoat large enough to cover my bulge and climbed into my bed, pulling the sheets over my head and wondering how long it would take me to sleep. I ignored my amma's shriek to go to the dining table. I know she is not the one to give up. She came with hot rice mixed with yoghurt and a large amount of pickle and she wondered if I needed some sambar. Snubbing her, I simply gulped what she had given and dozed off, having taken a decision.

At the breakfast table, Kaveri sits on the chair, pulls her knees to her bulge, and covers it with the stretched kurta top. Ever since Kaveri had come to know of the death of Athreya, she has become unruly with her conversation style and tone, especially with her mother. Lalitha and Venkat are sitting on a sofa, sharing sections of the newspaper.

'I have decided to meet Athreya's parents,' Kaveri announces.

'In this state of health? Have you gone insane?' Her mother's voice raises an octave.

Venkat turns away to busy himself with something that didn't need doing and letting the mother and daughter sort out their differences.

'You know, my college mate, Susan, is in Hyderabad. She agreed to help me out.'

'Susan Joseph? That Kerala Christian girl? She settled in the US, I thought.'

'She is now Susan Mehta. She married a Gujarati pharma professional. They have twin girls. Her husband is a big shot in Dr Reddy's.'

'But how will you search for Athreya's parents?'

Before Kaveri answers, Venkat says, 'I can accompany you, and we can stay in a hotel and do the search together.'

'I don't want to involve you guys at the moment. Susan will take care of me. She has a big apartment in a posh locality in Hyderabad with all the corporate perks of a car, driver, maid, cook and nanny. And she has taken a sabbatical from her employment to care for her young twins, so she is free to help me.'

'I'm curious as to why you want to embark on this journey. What if Athreya's parents disapprove of your relationship? It will strain you mentally and physically. Incidentally, what do you hope to accomplish by meeting them?'

Lalitha is visibly angry.

It is not a surprise: it is a statement Lalitha has come up with many times in the past three days, but having to repeat it is yet another reinforcement of her powerlessness against Kaveri's stubbornness.

Lalitha, who can't see anything without her glasses, looks at her daughter with helplessness and wishes they could have the kind of friendship that other mothers and daughters have. Lalitha wants to inform her befuddled daughter that she may face insults when she meets Athreya's parents. But Kaveri has always made it impossible for Lalitha to say anything: she appears to be covered in the guilt of being an unwed mother, which she wishes to be free of. How did this chasm come about? Many times in the past week, Lalitha tried to tell her daughter: 'please don't exert yourself. It is not safe for the baby and you.' She could somehow stop her visit to the Morgue, giving the ruse of infection. Now this visit to Hyderabad is not just the complications of travelling to Hyderabad that is troubling her, but the conversation she would have with the parents of Athreya. What would Lalitha do if the same thing happened to her? A heavily pregnant lady comes to her door and announces the foetus growing in her has your son's genes. Lalitha couldn't imagine the situation.

* * *

Susan Joseph's parents were US citizens, and by being born in the US, she also became a US citizen. They didn't want their young daughter exposed to US culture, especially when she was a teenager. So they packed Susan to India to her grandmother in Kerala. Susan moved to Bengaluru to pursue engineering while her parents were busy with their medical professions in the US. Susan was my engineering college mate. She graduated in electronics before enrolling in my college's IT programme. That made her three years my senior, age-wise. We got along like we were twins. She outperformed me in every subject, and we had this amusing rivalry over who would win the gold medal in the final year. Susan was the clear winner. I finished third. We were both chosen for campus placements. She accepted a job at Facebook and relocated to Los Angeles, California. As a US citizen, it was easy for Facebook to post her at their Headquarters. She met Ambrish Mehta in Los Angeles while he was on a business trip. They married in Los Angeles, per her parents' wishes, but moved to Hyderabad, India, where her husband worked for a global pharmaceutical company. She is currently on sabbatical, caring for her twins and has yet to decide whether to return to Facebook or look for another job in India.

She is said to have visited me while I was in a coma and spent the entire day beside my bed reminiscing about our college days. She continued to check with my amma about my recovery status. When I almost recovered, it seemed that Susan wanted to talk to me, but my parents denied permission as I might relapse. She was also unaware of my pregnancy status, as my parents avoided the embarrassing (!) topic.

When I called Susan last week, she sounded very concerned about me and wanted to come to Bengaluru to see me. I explained to her the entire sequence of events that led to my becoming pregnant and in a coma. I heard a choked voice at the other end. I told her the time had come to visit her instead and briefed her about my plan to meet Athreya's parents in Hyderabad.

I flew in from Bengaluru the previous evening. She picked me up from Airport in her large coffee-brown Hyundai Creta. I could see what ostentatious living means: Plasma Screen TV, computerised fridge, double-glazed windows to prevent noise pollution from outside, and branded toilet accessories, the works. Having been tired on the flight and long home-airport-home road travel at both ends, I decided to rest early and proceed with a plan we had discussed earlier on the phone. Susan's husband was on tour to the US, trying to canvass with USFDA for registration to inspect their new drug facility for commercial distribution in the United States. That made Susan relatively free to engage with me.

Sitting on her off-white modern sofa in a living room decorated with paintings, Susan talks while her twins are engaged by their nanny. We are polishing our plans to locate Athreya's parents.

'We know her name is Bhanumati, and she is a professor of economics working in a college. Beyond that, we know nothing.' Susan shuffles the cards.

'Can Google help us find commerce and economics colleges in Hyderabad?'

'As she is a professor, our list narrows to PG colleges,' says Susan, 'but indeed, the Universities also have departments of Economics, and there are more than three universities where Economics is likely to be taught. Also, we could add NALSAR University of Law too.'

'Can't we simply phone them and check?'

'We may try. The call will go to the PBX central station, and the operator will ask for an extension to connect. The operator would have no access to the staff names – she would only know the extension number. Some exchanges have a call-in mechanism, which may direct you to a receptionist or a faculty room to assist. But that is highly unlikely given the universities' shoestring budgets. But we shall try that too. That's a bit risky, though, the operator may connect us directly with Bhanumati. We decided that talking to Bhanumati in the work environment is not advisable given the sensitive matter.'

'So, that means we must visit every University and PG college in the city?'

'Yes. But we shall take our time. PG colleges are located in the city and are not a problem. It is the universities, situated in the outskirts of the city, which are a hassle of travel.'

'It's okay,' I say. A Mission is a mission.

'What if we bump into her unexpectedly? "Bhanumati, two young women are looking for you." And we are face-to-face with her.'

'It will be a disaster. We can't meet Bhanumati in public for the first time. That is why I plan to avoid the buildings or floors where faculty rooms and class sections are situated.'

'Then?'

'We shall always look for the Establishment Section or Admin Block. We need only to know that she works in that college. We have to get the contact number from the registry. That is all.'

We are ready with the plan and rehearse various possible scenarios. In unexpected situations, Susan said we have to improvise. I know she is good at it.

Susan contacts some of her friends who are born Hyderabadis and compiles a list of colleges and universities we should visit. We take up the University of Hyderabad, Gachibowli, as our first visit. Google maps take us to the Admin wing of the humongous campus of the University. As we ride through the University, we find its biodiversity amazing. We are led to the establishment wing and draw a blank on Bhanumati. We spent some time under a neem tree shade on a student's suggestion and ordered coffee from the nearby café. I could also find a way to unburden my bladder in the canteen's restroom as the trip from Susan's home to University was long.

Half a day has already gone, and amma has been worried as she called me umpteen times to check on my health.

We decide to go home and, after lunch, restart our search. The evening explorations in Dr Ambedkar College and two more PG colleges are of no avail. We closed our hunt for the day and resolved to renew our pursuit the next day.

Osmania University has an impressive campus with a large area of greenery, creating a relaxed atmosphere. Each discipline has its own building on the Univ estate. The Arts college building has an iconic status with its pinkish granite stone. It is a heritage structure, we are told. Until the IT revolution took over and the Cyber Towers in Madhapur became the modern Hyderabad image, the pics of Osmania Arts College and Charminar were the symbols that defined Hyderabad.

We needed human intervention to lead us, as signage was missing. We ask the passer-by for directions. We finally arrive at a modern-looking single-story admin building.

We're probably a bit early for the building to come to life. The Administration building appears to be a ghost bungalow with no one on the premises. Hyderabadis are known for their laid-back attitude.

We sit outside on a stone bench on the sidewall of the building near the cafeteria, which caters to those who visit the Admin building and nearby Printing Press. A young teenage boy hands over a laminated menu sheet with an infectious smile.

'Can I get you something? The tea here is the best in town.'

We order two teas. The boy brings two glasses of tea with a plate full of cookies. Susan tells me that it is the custom in Hyderabad that whenever Chai is requested, the café always delivers an assortment of the choicest biscuits whether you order or not. You pay only for those which you consume. We indulge in small talk with the boy. He is in the ninth grade in a school run by the University for the staff's children. We inquire as to why he is not attending school. He says that his mother is ill and that he is only here for one day. Otherwise, the café is run by his mother and her sister. Their husbands, who were on their payroll as Drivers, died in an unfortunate accident while taking the students to a picnic. The University Management allowed these ladies to operate a canteen on compassionate grounds. Our visit to the Salary section of the Admin block yields no result. It takes close to two hours to get this information, which would take ten minutes in an efficient working environment.

Our next visit is to Nizam's college. Their poorly designed web portal tells us that Nizam College is one of the oldest and most esteemed institutions of higher education in South India. The buildings were developed in Islamic architecture with inverted Lotus domes. We noticed graffiti of all hues on the building walls, which bore testimony to student activism. While having coffee at the college canteen, we met a couple of young students who saw our sober and homely dress and asked whether we were alumni of the college. We reply in the negative The Blue shirt says, 'Sorry to intrude, then why are you here?'

Susan chooses to reply.

'We are from Bengaluru and are on a vacation trip. Someone told us a visit to this college is a must, especially since we are academicians.' You must give it to Susan. She is clever.

'That is interesting. Did you visit all the departments? Did you meet any faculty members?'

'We came to soak in the atmosphere. Could you please tell us about the changes in college campus activities from the earlier years to now?'

The White shirt replies, 'In the seventies and right into late eighties, the institute was a cauldron of politics. You see the ground there where students are playing football. It used to be the public meeting place for political rallies. Many political careers were launched and buried here. Students used to be divided along ideological lines. Now we don't allow such political activism. However, we are presently in the thick of a different kind of activism: Climate Change, Women empowerment, Minority enablement and the like. Incidentally, our annual college fest is the best in South India. We are also proud of our alumni's accomplishments. Rakesh Sharma, the astronaut, is a graduate of this institution.'

'That's interesting,' I say and get up to move on, as we drew blank here too.

According to Google, our next destination, Osmania University College for Women, is in Koti, south of Hyderabad. This is one college affiliated with the University but is located outside the campus area. Later, during our interaction with a few students idling on the lawns, we learned that it is popularly known as Koti Women's College.

As we enter the college, we notice that the entry gate is only half open, allowing security to check the passengers of vehicles entering the premises. When the security guard notices all the occupants as females, he lets us go, sweeping the gates open. We follow the directions of a studious-looking man wearing thick-lens spectacles to the classroom section. We are now in a modern building with a glass dome and a large but vacant open area in the middle with an ornate staircase. To the right and left of the central location are two large decorative doors labelled Laboratories and Library. The floors are marble, and the stairwell is grey granite with a metal handrail. After a few moments, we see an older man with white hair and a thick file under his arm emerge from the left and walk briskly across the hallway to the outside premises. His demeanour clearly shows that he has been with the college for a long time. We walk calmly in front of him, much to his chagrin. And then wait for him to stop and ask, 'Sir, we've come to meet Madam Bhanumati, Professor of Economics. Could you please direct us to her?'

Earlier attempts to locate Bhanumati in various institutes resulted in referrals to a Personal Secretary to the Registrar, a Canteen Cook, and a Maid. So we decided to include her designation while we inquired about her.

In all searches, all investigations, whatever and wherever one needs a lucky break. Kaveri was going to get one.

The Oldman looks at us as if we are asking whether the sun rises in the east or west and says she could be in the classroom or the faculty room before walking away calmly. Our joy knows no bounds. We express our gratitude to the man, who appears surprised by our quick recognition of what seems to him to be a common-sense answer. We retrace our steps back to the main building, known as the Administration Block. We discover that the Oldman has not stopped staring at us as he walks towards his destination.

We want to avoid running into Bhanumati at work. Our only goal is to verify that Bhanumati is indeed employed at this college.

We now decide to carry out the next phase of our plan.

The administration building is an aesthetically and architecturally significant historic structure. It has a six-pillar British-style façade with a porch for dignitaries' cars to disgorge their VIP guests right at the entrance. We are still unsure of our final destination. We seek assistance, and a jean-clad girl leads us upstairs to the salary section.

We enter a hall filled with randomly placed tables with desktop computers, a few of which are populated.

We find a large table and stand in front of it, assuming it belongs to a high-ranking officer. The man in the swivel chair, glued to his computer screen, looks up. He raises his head above the monitor to see two ladies in their late twenties and smiles. His hair is closely cropped and cleanly shaven. 'Yes, how can I assist you?' he says, staring.

'Sir, we are former students of Professor Bhanumati and would like to meet her,' Susan says.

'This is the administration wing; you must go to the faculty section to find her. Her department is on the fourth floor of the next building.'

His voice is thin as if it came from a deep well.

'We've been there; she's not in her room.'

'Then you have to wait to meet her. She may be in a class.'

'We checked. Bhanumati Madam is not in the college.'

That's a bluff. We don't want to meet her on the college premises as our meeting needs to be in a more pleasant atmosphere, not in a noisy and nosy faculty room. Our purpose is to find her address and meet her at her home. Susan's active mind created this drama. We gambled that this gentleman would not call our bluff. He doesn't.

'Then you better come tomorrow.'

'I'm leaving for the United States tomorrow and wanted to pay my respects to her before I go,' Susan says.

I nod in agreement to everything Susan says without uttering a word.

'I don't think I can help. You could meet Madam's colleagues in the faculty room and ask how you can meet her today,' he says in a conciliatory tone.

'It's almost 4 p.m., and all of her colleagues would have left the college by now. Do you have her phone number so we can talk and set up an appointment?'

He now stands to his full height, at least two standard deviations less than the average Indian male, and selects a box file to search. Then he realises he has a computer that may contain the necessary information and can be quickly retrieved. He replaces the file in the cabinet and returns to his computer screen.

We finally have the necessary contact number after waiting a few agonising minutes. We thanked the officer and left faster than we had come. We reach home, unwind, and prepare for Phase 3 of our plan.

Susan dials the number. She switches her phone to speaker mode. I'm told to listen and not even breathe heavily.

'Yes, who is this?'

'Good evening, madam; my name is Susan Joseph, your ex-student. I've come from the United States to pay my respects to you.'

'Is there a student with that name in my class? Which year did you graduate? Are you an undergraduate or a postgraduate student?'

This type of in-depth investigation could get us into trouble. Susan responds without answering her question.

'Madam, you have imparted your knowledge to many students like me. We all are indebted to you. I understand it will be difficult for you to place me after all these years; however, once you see me, you surely can recollect, I am confident.'

'Okay. You can meet me tomorrow in college before 11 a.m. after that, I will be busy,' Bhanumati says.

'Madam, please excuse me. I am leaving for LA tomorrow early morning flight. I have to meet you tonight. Please don't deny me the pleasure.'

'Oh, is that so? Where are you now?'

Susan gives Bhanumati her location. We are overjoyed that she is willing to see us now.

Susan instructs her children's nanny to stay put for the night, promising she will call her husband to persuade him to do without her for one night.

We're on our way now.

It's almost six o'clock in the evening, and the streets are bustling with weary-eyed commuters heading home from work, and we're among them, adding to their numbers.

Now I have greater confidence in the path I am pursuing. But what will I do if she shuts the door on us, physically and figuratively? Susan comforts me by holding my hand and squeezing it compassionately.

We would not have had to take this laborious and risky route to find Athreya's parents if the Hospital's PM department had not failed to retrieve the address of the deceased's parents when they handed over the body after the autopsy. Susan believes that most hospitals' record-keeping systems, both private and public, are pathetic.

I recall a project we worked on in our college on the Oracle platform, where we created a college alumni database. Even with the slowest CPU processing speed, we could retrieve any Alumni's required data and display it on the screen in 40-50 seconds.

We spend more than 45 minutes navigating Hyderabad's chaotic traffic. Bhanumati's apartment is part of a massive complex – A to K towers – that is almost like a mini-city. We can count each tower's nineteen storeys but not the number of apartments. Despite the fact that madam had given prior notice of our arrival, the driver was not permitted to go beyond a certain point. Susan argues with the security guard, pointing out my advanced pregnancy status and pleading with him to let us drive up to the block of our destination. He reluctantly agrees, noting that our destination address was E 1208 - E tower, twelfth floor and flat number eight.

We ring the bell and find an elderly lady facing us, wearing a printed lemon-yellow cotton saree with a matching blouse adorned with flower motifs and a two-rupee-sized bindi on her forehead. She smiles and opens the door fully to let us in.

We find ourselves in a large hall that has been tastefully decorated in contemporary style with wall-to-wall cabinets in shades of grey and white to give the space an exquisite elegance. The paintings by well-known artists that adorn the walls reflect the residents' sense of taste. A mini-dining table for four with a coloured checker design table cover and four mahogany wooden chairs is placed at the end of the hall. A flower vase with fresh flowers sits in the centre of the table. I don't see any pickle bottles, unlike in my house, only one salt and pepper shaker on a circular wooden tray.

I can hear furious typing coming from the adjacent room.

'Please sit,' she says politely, 'who among you two is Susan?'

Susan extends her hand and introduces me.

'The name Kaveri sounds familiar. Is it safe for you to travel in this condition?' she asks, referring to my baby bulge.

'We wanted to meet you. That was important for us,' says Susan.

'Would you like something to drink?'

We nod for water and take a sip.

'Can I use your restroom?' I ask Bhanumati, and instead of simply pointing out the restroom, she leads me there with warmth. Lady of compassion, I believe.

We should have met sooner. Athreya, you are a complete idiot!

We sink into the stylish wooden sofa set made of solid Sheesham wood. The beautiful bent design and side cushion give the sofa an elegant appearance. Bhanumati settles into the sofa's opposite single seater.

Susan begins, as we've practised a million times. 'Madam, we regret to inform you that neither of us is your student. We need to see you on a different mission.'

'Are you sales girls? I'll have to contact security. This is unethical.' A big and stern tone.

Bhanumati stands up suddenly with a stern look that says – you get out now, or I will throw you out.

'What's going on?' A booming voice asks. An elderly gentleman neatly dressed in all white and with silvery hair and a thin moustache enters. I could judge him to be Athreya's father.

'We've come to speak with you about Athreya, your son. Please take your seats,' Susan says without vacating the couch.

They both exchange glances and decide to listen to us calmly. I take over.

'My name is Kaveri, Sir. My father is a superintending engineer in Bengaluru Power Corporation, my mother runs a dance school, and I work as a Network specialist in a Baltimore-based Legal outsourcing company in Bengaluru. I understand you are already acquainted with one Mr Gaurinath Pandey, a partner in your son's company. I would appreciate it if you could get more information about me from him. He is now available on the phone to speak with you.'

I say as rehearsed. I pause.

Both parents appear chaotic and muddled.

Susan also introduces herself.

'Madam, Kaveri and I were classmates in our Information Technology course in Bengaluru. I work for Facebook in the United States, and after getting married, I relocated to Hyderabad. I am on sabbatical from Facebook because I have twins to care for. My Husband works for Dr Reddy's.'

'What is your husband's name? I work for Dr Reddy's as well,' Athreya's father inquires.

'Ambrish Mehta, He is in charge of obtaining USFDA approval for new drugs and formulations.'

'I know Mehta. In fact, we travelled to the United States several times together.'

That relieves some of our pressure because we could establish some credentials.

'Could you please tell me more about your relationship with my son?' asks Bhanumati, looking straight into my eyes. It appears that she is beginning to understand the reason for our visit.

I explain slowly, explicitly, and in detail the evolution of my and Athreya's official relationship into an intimate relationship during our work proximity.

'In fact, if it hadn't been for the torrential rain on February 10th, when you were in Bengaluru for a wedding, we would have met. Athreya arranged for us to meet when you were in Bengaluru. I was delayed at home due to a family emergency, and you left early for the airport due to rain delays on the road to the airport. It was Athreya's wish that our future relationship's decision be revealed to you in my presence.' I say with a lot of sincerity and conviction.

'Remember Bhanu, when we went to pick up our son's dead body, Gaurinath Pandey hinted at one other lady on pillion on the bike, and he insisted we meet the parents of the lady. We were a little embarrassed to present ourselves to them because we felt our boy was responsible for the situation the lady and her parents were in.'

It was Athreya's father who spoke softly in a simple explanatory voice.

'We went back after two weeks to pick up his belongings from the apartment, but it never occurred to us to meet the victim's parents,' Bhanumati reflects ruefully.

Susan says, 'I understand from Venkat uncle – Venkatraman is Kaveri's appa – that the morgue authorities, where your son's post-mortem was performed, preserved your son's DNA on uncle's insistence for future reference because Kaveri was in a coma at the time, and they were unable to ascertain the particulars of your son's address to contact you.'

I notice Bhanumati taking deep breaths.

'Do you mean to tell me that my son Athreya is the father of the child Kaveri is carrying?'

'The preserved DNA can demonstrate it,' I say and immediately regret it.

Athreya's parents look at each other. They ask a few more questions about my association with Athreya and his likes and dislikes, probably to confirm that our relationship is indeed intimate.

They invite us to stay for dinner, during which they learn about my family history and how my parents dealt with my coma condition.

'I can relate to your parents' anguish,' says Bhanumati, 'how long are you here in Hyderabad?'

'I am planning to leave tomorrow early morning flight,' I explain, 'I've already been here three days, much to my mother's annoyance. She forbade me from going out of Bengaluru alone. She insisted on escorting me, but I wanted to do it alone.'

'May I accompany you?' Bhanumati asks.

'It would be my pleasure to introduce you to my parents.' I try hard not to show my excitement.

'Wait a minute,' says Athreya's father, now introduced to us as Suryanarayana Rao. Susan and I stare at him as if he's about to drop a bombshell.

'Bhanu, we have another mission regarding the Salus Cyber Security Solutions' business. When we were about to leave for Hyderabad with the ambulance, Gaurinath wanted us to meet with all of the company's other partners and decide the company's future. Let us take advantage of this opportunity to complete this long-overdue task. I can speak with Gaurinath and set up a time during the upcoming weekend.'

That means I'll have to come along as well,' he adds.

'Sir ...' he cuts me off as I'm about to say something.

'Please do not address me as Sir, Uncle for you.'

'In fact, we have already informed Gaurinath that he be available on the phone to speak with you if we require his assistance. He's waiting for us to call,' I say.

I already took Gaurinath in confidence about my Mission-Athreya, as he named it. He is as interested in my pursuit as I am, as he explained later. His partner, Ganesan, appears to be having jitters about tackling their company clients. Also, their other partner Kothari is exerting pressure on them to decide on the future of the business now that Athreya, the founder, is not around.

On cue from everyone, I call Gauri and set up a Zoom call.

'Good day, everyone. Hello Suryanarayana Sir. Kaveri, how are you? Congratulations on embarking on such a daring mission,' Gauri is beaming as he addresses us.

I introduce him to Susan.

Suryanarayana assumes command.

'Mr Pandey, my wife Bhanumati, and I want to come to Hyderabad not only to meet Kaveri's parents but also to hear your team's thoughts on the future of Salus. We can move forward if you can arrange a meeting on Saturday with all of us, including your other partner, Ganesan.'

'Sure, sir, I will organise it. There is much uncertainty about the business's future direction, and with Kaveri around, we should be able to reach an agreement. Kothari, our other partner, is also putting pressure on us,' Gaurinath adds and bids goodbye to us all.

I profusely thank the parents of Athreya and take leave from them to meet at the Airport the next morning.

Chapter 20

Karnataka voters have returned a fractured verdict to their Legislative Assembly. No party got a majority to rule the state. The Governor has asked the incumbent government of the Pan India Party to run the administration till a new outfit is sworn in. There was no pre-poll alliance by any party. Every party was confident of a winning majority on its strength. Pan India Party (PIP) and Indian National Unity Party (INUP) are the two primary contenders for the throne.

Meanwhile, hectic parleys are going on between the opposition parties to keep the last government of PIP from getting to power again. After two weeks of meetings and media debates, INUP manages to persuade local and regional parties to agree to a common minimum program to bid for government formation. They succeed, and a new Government is sworn in. Not before candidates shifted allegiance to one alliance or the other as per the wind. Governor has used his discretion under article 163 of the Constitution, or some critics say a dice, to call INUP – which is also the ruling party at the centre to form the government with a proviso that the new government will face a floor test within ten days.

* * *

Gandharva Konnuru has become a member of the legislative assembly for the first time. He is on the right side of forty and had a ten-year stint as an IAS officer before he decided to plunge into politics.

His grandfather, Chinnakesava Konnuru, was a freedom fighter and rumoured to have been the jail mate of Savarkar in the Cellular Jail at Port Blair. While campaigning for his election, Gandharva had said, 'During the few years of service at the Indian Administration, I was unable to serve the people with satisfaction, as every scheme I designed for the welfare of the people is required to pass through politicians who had their stamp of authority which invariably diluted my sincere efforts. So, I thought the best way to serve the people is to join politics in the footsteps of my Grand Father.'

Gandharva doesn't get any ministerial berth. Media rumours indicated that he might shift to the other party. Sensing this dissatisfaction, the President of INUP called Gandharva personally that he would be accommodated in the next cabinet expansion. Will he accept the responsibility of the Chairmanship of Bengaluru Power Corporation, which needed some dynamic officer to lead the organisation, which of late is mired in controversies? Gandharva agrees. His first assignment, as given by the Central Leadership, is to ensure that the long pending Japanese Investment is moved on a fast track by providing all the infra needs are in place.

On a request from the Chairman, Venkatraman is |waiting in the ante-room to meet him. Venkat finds the room very shabby, with dirty drapes and peeling plaster. A middle-aged woman welcomes him and, after knowing his business, asks him to wait for the arrival of the Chairman. After a wait of over three-quarters an hour, the Chairman walks in. As soon as he is seated, he asks his secretary to send Venkat in.

'Good afternoon, Mr Venkatraman. I am sorry to have kept you waiting. The party meeting took longer than I anticipated,' said Gandharva.

'It's okay, sir.'

'Don't call me sir. You are much older than me.'

'I am not aware of the agenda of our meeting today. Otherwise, I would have asked my colleagues to join me.'

'I have deliberately not given a brief to you before our meeting. I wanted to have a one-to-one interface with you. Our government is worried about the delays in the Thimmalahalli Substation commissioning. I want to know the latest and how I can help push it through faster.'

'The substation is already commissioned. Because of an unfortunate accident, the court had directed the Disciplinary Committee to order a forensic analysis of the incident and report.'

'Who went to court on the matter?'

'The opposition party, that is INUP, in which your party is also a coalition partner.'

'At that time, I was not part of INUP. This arrangement of coalition with INUP is to ensure there is no need for a fresh election, the cost of which we can ill afford,' said Gandharva, 'So, the final investigative report and the findings of the Disciplinary Committee have been submitted to the government?'

'Yes. It is pending with the Government. They must submit to the court and request the court to vacate the stay, so the unit is re-commissioned.'

'Okay. I shall take it up separately. I read the full background of the contract and the issues about poor supervision at the site. A newspaper report attached to the file shows that the contractor is not experienced in such construction works. How far is that true?'

Venkat is in a bind. If he exposes the connections of the previous Chairman, the then Minister for Power and the Contractor, he would not be able to substantiate. On the contrary, he might be vilified. Can't really go back and correct the choices we made.

'Mr Gandharva, the erection of the substation is exactly as per the specifications given in the contract. So to that extent, we can't blame the contractor. Of course, he compromised the connectivity to the Earthing Grid, which resulted in the accident. But such errors don't occur often, and even if they do, it rarely involves the loss of human life. This case is a one-off. That is what we had explained to the DC.'

'As per the documents I have, it is learnt that the Contractor – Bhogam Constructions, was not originally declared L1. How come he got the contract?'

'Yes. The contractor was L2. But, L1 refused to sign the agreement for construction. So we had to request L2 perforce to accept L1 rates and sign the contract, which he did. As you know, we had a time constraint because of the proposed Japanese Investment and the pressure from the Central Government. If L2 had also refused the acceptance of the rates of L1, we had to retender, which meant a loss of precious time,' says Venkat.

'As per the records, the Tender Committee approved the award of the Contract to L1 in Nov 2018. TC has passed on to your department, requesting you get the contract signed by L1 and proceed with the work. And you did not invite the L1 to sign the contract till Jan 2019, nor have you issued the LOI, as is the norm. By the time you asked the L1 contractor to start work, the validity period was over, and the contractor was in his right to renege on his quotation.'

Venkat notices a petulant edge to the Chairman's voice. He could feel where this conversation was going. He has to tread carefully. Venkat has no proof of his meetings with the CE and MD wherein he was directed to hold the contract to L1 to favour L2.

'During that period, we had four Tenders in the final stages. We were short of staff. My department has only one AE, and he was on leave. The agreements and contract specs needed a technical background; commerce clerks couldn't handle such details. So all the call letters got delayed. But I am sure that this particular invitation letter had gone to L1 much earlier than the expiry of the validity period. I have to check that. I understand that the government at that time investigated the matter after media reports and did not find any lapse on this count from my office.' I had to bluff.

'Can you send me the copy of the initial call letter and date of posting from the tappal records of your office so that I can verify your claim?'

Venkat lets one beat of silence pass before he replies.

Venkat has to divert the conversation away from his alleged complicity. Had the accident not happened, this matter would not have been blown out of proportion. Now the way the Chairman is taking the issue, he could be made a scapegoat. He has to put the ball in the Chairman's court to divert.

'Sure. Meanwhile, if you can use your good offices to vacate the stay by the court, we can undertake corrective actions on the substation so it can be re-commissioned immediately.'

'Yes, I shall. How long will the unit be re-commissioned once I get the stay vacated?'

'Just one week. All the required testing is already in place. The contract for the new fence is also given. We have to give the go-ahead to the contractor to start work.'

'Okay, thanks. Please keep me in the loop on matters in this work. This project is not a routine one. You very well know the importance of this substation.'

They say goodbye to each other, and Venkat leaves the room, contemplating how to avoid detailed scrutiny of the L1 to L2 transfer of the contract. He knows fully well that he doesn't have any documented record of the directives of the then Chairman, MD and CE. He could be in trouble.

* * *

On a call from the Inspector, Lalitha and Venkat visit the police station.

'Are you sure that the car you had seen standing in front of your office for four days is that of the accused?' asked Manjunatha.

Lalitha senses that she is supposed to answer in the affirmative. She nods.

'Our investigations have not revealed any such sightings. There is no evidence available. No CC TV cameras in your street. Our constable has inquired with the neighbours and the opposite house residents, who have not seen any such SUV.'

'I am sure of that,' Lalitha says weakly.

Manjunatha says, 'I told you that we need evidence to buttress your assertion about the possible involvement of this SUV in the accident.'

'Yes, you did,' affirms Venkat.

'I also told you that if we don't find any proof, we may have to file a motion to dismiss the FIR – rather withdraw the FIR. Before I say anything, you need to understand the nature of a charge sheet, which is the consequence of an FIR. No law says you can't file a case full of holes. We did that. We must find some substantive merit in following up on the FIR. There is no evidence that Karthik was stalking you, as he did two decades ago, by planting himself across your house. Also, there is no way for Karthik to know that the lady on the bike is your daughter, though the resemblance is striking. Hence there is no motive established for Karthik to hurt your daughter as revenge against you, either deliberately or accidentally. You have shown evidence from a private camera recording of his going along the same street behind your daughter and retracing back. That does not prove his car hit the bike intending to kill her or by negligence. The one witness at the site of the accident, who called the ambulance and us, did not report any other vehicle near the accident site. However, he referred to a person in a security guard uniform running away from the site. We presumed that he was the person who stole the mobile and wallet from the person of the male victim.'

Venkat speaks without letting Lalitha open her mouth.

'What is the best course now? We made an error, and we don't want to be hauled up for misleading the Police and framing an innocent.'

'I can help by filing a closure report under section 169 of CrPC. There are three types of closure reports. "A" summary, wherein the Police could not find enough evidence. "B" summary, wherein we file that the complaint is maliciously fake. "C" summary is when a case is neither true nor false and is filed due to a mistake. If I file a "B" summary, Karthik's father, a reputed and no-hold-barred lawyer, may come hammer and tongs against you. "A" summary does not close the FIR and is open for future investigation, and in this case, that would be a waste of our minimal resources. "C" summary is the only way to save you.'

'Thank you,' Venkat says.

'Wait. That is not so simple. I have to take Sheshadri into confidence so that he does not file a defamation case against you. I hope to convince him as I had not arrested his son, though I was in my right to do so without a warrant as the FIR shows it as a cognisable offence. I sympathise with madam with her two-decade-old memories of stalking that affected her psyche, and all her anger is the result of the unforgettable past incidents.'

What does he know about my pain due to Karthik's obsession and subsequent police case? Because of which, I was frustrated as I couldn't pursue my passion.

Venkat rises from his seat, holds Inspector's hands, and says, 'We are forever thankful to you. Some debts can never be paid.'

All this time, Lalitha is silent and does not utter a word as though she came rehearsed, anticipating this scenario.

While returning from the PS, Venkat says, 'We have our daughter back in good health. Let us be happy about it. Please bury your obsession with that rascal and enjoy our Grandparent status.'

Venkat has enough on his plate to bother about his wife's fixation on an event that happened two decades ago.

Epilogue

Lalitha could not accept her loss of the opportunity to become a renowned scientist. She subtly held everyone around her and society accountable for her predicament. She would sulk whenever she saw media reports praising the accomplishments of women like Indira Nooyi, Kiran Mazumdar Shaw, and Hillary Clinton, among others. And it would cause her to lose her cool. Her husband and her daughter bore the brunt of her wrath. Although her dance school was popular in Bengaluru and the United States, she was always missing her adulthood ambition.

Kaveri gave birth to a healthy boy. He was given the name Atharva. The child was cared for by both grandparents in turn. Athreya's parents relocated to Bengaluru to be closer to their grandson and to allow Kaveri to focus on her career.

Atharva looked much like Athreya. He appeared to be a copy, a clone, if you will. He even has the same skin tone as Athreya. Bhanumati frequently stated that her grandson resembled Athreya when he was 1 to 3 months old, including his smile. 'I'm willing to bet that if I show you a picture of Athreya when he was 1 to 3 months old, you'll think it's Atharva,' she said.

Venkatraman escaped an investigation into the deceptive changes he made to award the contract to Bhogam Constructions. The unexpected change in government aided as the previous political ensemble retook government control. Venkatraman and his team's fence design has become an Industry standard for all substations.

Kaveri quit her job and joined Salus Cyber Security Solutions to pursue Athreya's ambition. Gaurinath Pandey couldn't come to accept a full-time assignment at Salus but continued to assist Kaveri and her team, moonlighting while working for Wipro. The company successfully sold its FIREWALL systems across many countries through Kaveri's marketing and Ganesan's technical efforts. Salus Firewall had become the default bundle in ACAROID, the popular mobile operating system.

References

1. Legal Opinion on Medical Termination of Pregnancy: https://bit.ly/3NQ0ZQZ
2. Pregnant Woman in Coma Is Focus of Abortion Debate https://nyti.ms/3G3xhpy
3. Coma in Pregnancy – Neurology Clinic report https://bit.ly/3tfNLTU
4. Coma: Causes etc. (medicalnewstoday.com) https://bit.ly/3WNI90Q
5. COMA and Glasgow Scale https://bit.ly/3WNI90Q
6. Aruna Shanbagh Case https://bit.ly/3X1OlTh
7. The Brain May Repair Itself – TED Lecture https://bit.ly/3UDEFMo
8. Guardianship for Coma Patients – court ruling http://bit.ly/3UOpn7F
9. Signs of Improvements in coma patients http://bit.ly/3UxV1Xl

10. Earthing and Grounding in Electric Substations

http://bit.ly/3UxFFSS

11. Safety Practices in Substations

http://bit.ly/3hDHPBT

12. What killed the Goat

http://bit.ly/3Gft5n3

13. Improper Earthing hazards

http://bit.ly/3X0yzrM

14. Six Simple rules for Substation safety

http://bit.ly/3tpyKit

15. Why Substation Equipment fail

http://bit.ly/3TtV9FV

16. Fencing Systems for Substations

http://bit.ly/3hFOUS8

17. Proper Fencing – by Kerbing

http://bit.ly/3Twh5Ac

18. Karnataka Power Corporation – departmental disciplinary action – court judgement

http://bit.ly/3O2FeNI

19. Aliant Energy – Substation fencing with barbed wire

20. NSW TRANSPORT RAIL CORPORATION – Substation fencing specifications

To My Readers

Malcolm Gladwell, the celebrated author of The Tipping Point, referring to the aggregate society, had said: "any number of mysterious changes mark everyday life." Such oddities occur in personal life too, and they can significantly alter the course of one's life. These quirks are referred to as karma by Hindus, allowing them to cope with the vagaries of life. I encourage my readers to share the unexpected turns (tipping points) in their lives that have made a significant difference in their lives. **velury17@gmail.com** is my email address.

www.ingramcontent.com/pod-product-compliance
Lightning Source LLC
LaVergne TN
LVHW010055170826
845678LV00012B/2150

* 9 7 9 8 8 8 8 6 9 6 4 6 0 *